UNCONDITIONALLY YOURS

Ciara McMahon

© 2009 Ciara McMahon

All rights reserved. No part of this publication may be reproduced in any form or by any means—graphic, electronic or mechanical, including photocopying, recording, taping or information storage and retrieval systems—without the prior written permission of the author.

978-1-907179-46-4

A cip catalogue for this book is available from the National Library.

Published by Original Writing Ltd., Dublin, 2009.
Printed by Cahill Printers Limited, Dublin

DEDICATIONS

To all who refuse to give up hope in the face of adversity.

He spun and fell and spun again and fell a thousand times,

In though he fell he rose again, and once again he tried.

ACKNOWLEDGEMENTS

To Angela M, Angela G, Nessa and my mammy for reading this when it was a stream of words without any punctuation not an easy thing.

To Steven and Garrett for all your work on this manuscript.

THANK YOU.

I

Claire stared from her desk through the frosted glass of the door that opened into the accounts office. She could see the man in the helmet climbing the stairs. *Sweet Jesus no not again she thought. Please let it be a package from DHL or something.* The man opened the door and she could see the huge display of flowers he carried in his hand in the plastic bag of water.

"She's there", said Adrian, pointing to Claire before the delivery man could ask.

"Can you sign there," he asked passing a clip board to Claire.

"What's this", said Ashley "lads come look he must have been paid again today". Catriona came out of the office. "See that there Tom how come you never send me flowers at work"?

"Because I work with you love, said Tom, and live with you I must be a saint".

"The cheek of you", said Catriona.

"So what does he keep doing wrong that he keeps sending you all these flowers, or what are you doing to keep him on his toes like this"? asked Adrian.

"What sweets do we have today"? said Ashley, oh Lir ok but tell him that I preferred the whole basket of muffins thing. Tell him to do that again".

"So, said Tom, you still haven't told us how you keep all these gifts coming have you a gold pussy or what"?

"Oh shut up said Claire you dirty bastard".

"Yeah you tell him, said Catriona, see what I have to put up with".

"You're so lucky, said Ashley.

Yeah, said Adrian, he treats you like a princess". "He's a keeper for sure", said Catriona.

"Jesus", said Claire, "ye can have him the thick fucker even at work I can't get away from him I'd swear he is out on that building site sniffing the fumes from the glue or the petrol or oil or something". "Either that or he is on the whacky backy without me knowing". "Here", said Claire, "who wants those flowers or will I throw them in the bin"?

"It's my turn", said Tom. "Here Catriona love", he said handing them to her."Don't ever say I don't give you flowers at work again".

Catriona laughed, "cheap skate", she said poking Tom with the flowers.

Claire passed the sweets to Adrian. "Do you want one"? "Help yourselves", she said opening the box and placing it on the desk.

"Claire", said Ashley, "does Matthew never ask why you don't ever bring the flowers home"?

"No", said Claire, "he thinks it's sweet of me to give the flowers to people with no one to give them flowers". "I told him I donate them to people in hospital with no one to visit them he thinks I'm next in line to mother Theresa".

"Wow", said Catriona, "what do you say to that"? "Awe", said Adrian, "listen to the card".

"What does it say"? Tom asked. "It says counting the hours until evening love as always Matthew".

"So what's that we have now", said Adrian as she pulled the other cards from the top drawer of her desk. "I love keeping these cards do you know what they remind me of those little sweets I can't remember their names but they had little love notes on them". "Oh, I know the ones you mean", said Ashley, "love hearts".

"Oh yeah I loved those sweets to", said Catriona, "I wonder can you still get them were those the ones that fizzed in your mouth when you sucked them?"

"I don't think so", said Tom. "You know what I loved was those apple jacks".

"Shush", said Catriona, "I want to listen to the cards".

"Go on Adrian", said Ashley.

"Ahem", said Adrian, clearing her throat. "Just to brighten up you day", love Matthew. "Thinking of you every second I breathe, love always Matthew".

"That there is my favorite you know", said Catriona. "No keep going", said Ashley, "I like the one about the lilies".

"Oh that's my favorite to," said Adrian, as she rooted through the hundreds of cards in the drawer. "Ah here it is cream lilies white and pure just to say I'm always yours know that you are my better part, love always Matthew". "You're so lucky", said Adrian. "I'd do anything to find someone like that who lives to make me feel special".

"Yeah", said Ashley and Catriona.

"Well", said Claire, "ye are welcome to the thick fool he wrecks my head take those flowers out of my face Catriona if you want them before I throw them in the bin". "Bitch", said Catriona, picking up her bunch of irises lilies and red roses, and taking them into her office for safe keeping.

Matthew lay awake staring at the red numbers on the screen of the alarm clock listening to the howling wind blowing the rain against the window. Five minutes left before the alarm would go off. He felt the warmth of Claire's body cuddled up against him, and smiled. *A day for the fire and television, thought Matthew.* Claire turned in her sleep and put her arm around him. Beep, beep, beep went the alarm. Immediately Matthew turned the radio alarm from buzz to off. He didn't want to wake Claire she didn't work Monday's. Matthew wasn't going into work himself either. Not until after lunch. He was going to organize an anniversary present for Claire. Matthew went downstairs and turned on the radio. The breakfast show was on. Matthew put on the kettle and put a tea bag in a mug took milk from the fridge and popped two slices of toast under the grill. The kettle bubbled and then clicked off. Matthew made himself a cup of tea and sat down listening to the radio and had his breakfast. Next he went upstairs and had a shower. He went into the bedroom wrapped in a towel to grab his clothes.

Claire sat up in the bed, "hi honey I never heard you get up". "It's a terrible day out there I whish you didn't have to go to work in that".

Matthew went over and sat on the bed beside Claire. "You're not getting up on any roofs today are you"? Claire asked. "You'll be blown off".

Matthew laughed. "Don't worry babe I'll be fine I'm in doors doing kitchens at the minute anyways".

"I wish you could stay at home for the day", said Claire; "we could sit in front of the fire and watch the television". "That would be lovely babe and I wish I could but the way things are at the moment I can't afford to be taking days off".

"I know", said Claire. Matthew looked over at the clock. "Jesus Claire, half eight the time flies in the morning I better get dressed and go". Matthew went over to the wardrobe and pulled out a jumper shirt and jeans. "I have to do a few things in town this morning before I go into work". "Is there a bag I can put my work clothes in to take them with me"? Claire went to get out of bed to get Matthew a bag. "Don't get up babe", said Matthew, "tell me where it is and I'll go get it myself". "There's a sports bag in the blanket box at the end of the bed", said Claire.

"Nice one babe if I'm still in town at lunch time I'll give you a ring". He walked over to the bed and kissed Claire.

"Do babe I'll just be home here doing nothing bored," said Claire.

"Right honey I'll talk to you later I better head", said Matthew. Claire turned over in the bed and went back to sleep and Matthew put on his jacket got in the car drove into town and parked in the all day car park. That hour of the morning he probably would have got a parking space in the town but he was more than happy to walk put off for a few more minutes the time he would arrive at Claire's work place.

Matthew stared up at the narrow stairs that lead to Claire's office, he felt nervous he hated asking anyone for anything, his stomach was tied in knots, and he felt sick. He wished he didn't have to do this. What if she said no then he would be so disappointed it would show on his face they would see it. What if he got tears in his eyes, what if she laughed at him or worse still what if she got cross and started roaring and shouting at him? But the only way he could avoid asking was to get Claire to ask, and if he asked Claire to do that it would ruin the surprise. Matthew willed his feet to move and climbed the tiny stairs that led to the office. There were five desks scattered around a big room with an office with a glass door at the back. Matthew recognized one of the girls she had been up to the house with Claire.

"Hi Ashley, I've an appointment to see Catriona", said Matthew.

"Oh dead on she's in the office there".

"Will you tell her I'm here", asked Matthew?

"Jesus", said Ashley, "where dya think you are just go in don't want her head getting any bigger than it already is now do we"?

"I heard that", roared Catriona out the door.

"You were supposed to", replied Ashley.

"Hi Matthew what can I do for you?" asked Catriona.

"Well", said Matthew, "I hope you don't think it ignorant of me to ask, but I was hoping that I could maybe, only if it doesn't put you out, I know it's short notice like it's ok if you can't and I hope I'm not over stepping the mark, and I hope it will be ok with you either way not to tell Claire I was here". Matthew moved nervously from one foot to another, taking tiny steps over and back. He never noticed the three legged stool in front of him he stumbled forward over it and landed on his knees on the floor.

"Jesus", said Catriona, "I'm sorry Matthew I can't marry you bigamy isn't legal yet but if you'd consider moving to one of those countries where you can have as many wives as you like I'd strongly consider it".

Matthew laughed and dusted the dirt from his knees as he got up from the floor; "I'm mortified could I make a bigger fool of myself".

"Your ok", said Catriona, what can I do for you?"

"I hate asking anyone for a favor but you see next week is Valentines Day and our first years wedding anniversary and I was hoping to take Claire on a two week cruise of the Caribbean to celebrate only of course if it was possible with you to give her the two weeks off and also can you say nothing to Claire it's a surprise".

"Oh my God, said Catriona, I never thought a man like you existed and was this all your own idea or did someone else put it into your head?"

"No, no, said Matthew I thought of it myself". "Right one more question before I say yes", said Catriona, tell me this have you a brother?"

Matthew laughed. "So", he asked, is it possible?

"Yeah, yeah it's no bother at all Claire only works two days a week anyway so we will only be short four days in two weeks". "Oh thank you so much", said Matthew, "this means so much to me you don't know how much I really want our first years anniversary to be special see I reckon we will have children to think of from this year out".

"What's this, asked Ashley?"

"Oh", said Catriona this man here just wants me to give his wife two weeks holidays so he can whisk her off on a cruise of the Caribbean".

"Oh my God", said Ashley, "see if ye ever break up call me". They all laughed.

"Well", said Matthew, "I better head and book this cruise or else we won't be going anywhere".

"Oh my God", said Ashley to Catriona when Matthew was gone, "that jammy bitch and all she ever does is give out about him".

"That is none of our business", said Catriona, "but yeah you're right she doesn't know how lucky she is".

Matthew bounced off the street delighted with himself as the rain bounced off the path around him. He thought back to when he and Claire had met. They had met whilst he and his best friend Dave were in Thailand; they had like the rest of the country taken a year out to travel. Claire and Matthew had kept contact by email throughout their travels and they met up again in Australia and climbed Ayer's rock together.

Matthew stared at the height of the rock and felt palpitations I hope to god I don't have to climb that he remembered thinking like it was yesterday, and then the sigh of relief he took when the guide had said the rock was sacred to the Aboriginal people and it was preferred you didn't climb it. The perfect out clause he had thought. He watched as everyone else in the group turned to walk towards the rock. Claire had turned to him so are we going up? Maybe we should leave it babe Matthew had said. We should show respect. But, Claire had said I want to be able to say I climbed it when I go home. Ok so Matthew had said even from the start he could never say no to Claire. So Matthew climbed the rock with her, and for the first time in his life his fear of heights didn't bother him nothing was an obstacle with Claire by his side. She was his missing piece in a puzzle that spent years incomplete. Now that he had found that missing piece he worshipped the picture his life had become.

I wonder why that came into my head now; I must ring Dave this evening and see how he is thought Matthew. He worried for his friend Dave that bookies shop has been nothing but trouble ever since he's opened it he'll end up without a roof over his head yet because of it. Matthew turned down the narrow streets that lead to the travel agents Travels. The shop was the most colorful in the town. The front of the shop was covered in murals depicting different scenes from the many lands encountered by Gulliver on his travels. Well thought Matthew I hope our cruise isn't as eventful as all that as he looked at the mural of Gulliver tied to the ground and surrounded by thousands of Lilliputians. Matthew walked into the travel agents, it was lovely and warm. There were two leather sofas with end tables holding travel books hard back copies, at either side of an old black cast iron fireplace there were six candles sitting on the floor in the fireplace tall ones to the back smaller ones to the front they flickered in the grate as their scent wafted pleasantly around the room. There was a boiler surrounded by large colorful mugs with colorful saucers. They reminded Matthew of those used by the Mad Hatter and March hare at Alice in wonderlands tea party. There were two wicker baskets one held sachets of coffee cappuccinos mochas lattés and regular coffee the other held hot chocolate mint, orange, milk and dark chocolate flavor all healthy options. There was a small fridge with a glass door sitting beside the mugs with tiny single serving cartons of milk and freshly whipped cream. There were two ladies in the shop. Matthew walked up to the counter and sat in one of the three leather recliner chairs in front of the desk. "Hi", said one of the ladies behind the desk, "I'm Justine, how can I help you?"

"Hi", said Matthew, "this shop is lovely its nicer than most of the coffee shops in town and the fireplace I'd say you get people coming in here just to sit down and relax".

"Oh thank you", said Justine, "I'm the owner I designed the décor myself I redo it with the seasons I want people to feel like the holiday experience starts when they walk through the door you know last summer I had non alcoholic cocktails and baskets of rock candy".

"They had to be non alcoholic because they drank all the quantro and vodka while they were decorating the place", shouted a girl who Matthew thought to be about fifteen years old from the end of the counter.

"Shut your mouth and eat your lunch", Justine replied, "or you can go back to school altogether". "I want this shop to be different", Justine continued, "I want people to enjoy booking their holiday here so they will hopefully come back".

"Well I'm very impressed so far anyway", said Matthew, "how long are you here now?" "We're here almost a year now", *would you look at those big blue eyes thought Justine I'd hit that.* "So said Justine, do you want to look through some brochures?"

"Well", said Matthew, "I have something in particular in mind I'd love to book a cruise of the Caribbean for myself and my wife Claire for two weeks".

Should have known thought Justine all the good ones gay or taken.

"On Valentines Day", said Matthew, "it's our anniversary so it's extra special for us". "I'm just hoping I can keep the surprise for the week and don't ruin things I'm so excited".

"So", said Justine, "your wife knows nothing about this that's so sweet". "You know you'll need her passport to book this?"

"Yeah I thought I might", said Matthew, "I have it here".

"Your organized", said Justine, taking both passports from Matthew she quickly flicked the top one open she was always curious to see peoples passport photos first Matthews well that was a very good picture, then Claire's. "She's very beautiful this wife of yours no wonder you spoil her", said Justine, "now let's take a look on the computer and see what we can find you". "Right I can get you on a cruise leaving Dublin on the fifteenth I'm afraid there's nothing available leaving on the fourteenth". "Jesus", said Justine it's not cheep three thousand euros each do you want me too see if I can find you something else other than a cruise?"

"No, no", said Matthew, "it's always been Claire's dream to go on a cruise ever since she was a little girl watching the love boat and I want this to be perfect".

"Lucky Claire", said Justine.

"Ah she's very good to me too", said Matthew, "she's my life I don't know what I'd do with out her".

Justine smiled, "fine so I am more than happy to relieve you of six thousand euro". *If he only knew how happy I am to take his money thought Justine, The year the Celtic tiger stopped roaring what a time to start a business.* Justine had an appointment with the bank manager coming up that she was dreading.

"Here", said Matthew, "pulling a credit card from his wallet put it on that". Matthew got his credit card back with a print out of their departure and arrival time and all the places they would visit on the way. On Sunday week they were flying from Dublin to Liverpool where they would be boarding their ship. Matthew left the shop and walked up the street, he was so happy and so excited nine days to go and we'll be boarding the ship and to think I was half afraid to ask Catriona if Claire could have the time off, when she couldn't have been nicer they are a lovely bunch of people Claire works with. We must bring them back a surprise. Matthew walked up the street delighted with himself he took out his mobile and called Claire.

"Hi honey how are you"? "Just thought I'd ring to say hello".

"Well you said it," said Claire.

"Ha, ha", said Matthew, "do you want to come down town and we can go for lunch". "Yeah, yeah, why not I've nothing else to do", said Claire.

"Great, great", said Matthew "I'll meet you in the diners delight so". Matthew headed down to the diners delight to meet Claire on the way down he passed a clothes shop in the window was a bag that Claire had told him she liked. *I'll give it to her at lunch for a surprise, thought Matthew.* He went into the shop he was shocked when he was told the price of the bag four hundred euros.

"Ah", said the girl, "but it comes with a free purse".

"Is it gold plated to boot", asked Matthew?

"Would you like it wrapped?" asked the lady in the shop.

"Yeah, yeah", said Matthew, "that would be great".

"Is it a Valentines Day gift", asked the lady?

"Nah", said Matthew, "I've that one sorted already".

"Oh", said the lady. *Jesus she thought some people have more money than sense.* Matthew left the shop and called Claire.

"What", said Claire, when she answered the phone?

"It's me honey", said Matthew.

"Yeah", said Claire, "I know who it is, is everything ok?"

"Yeah", said Matthew, "I'm just ringing you to let you know I'm not at the diners delight yet didn't want you sitting there wondering where I am".

"Matthew babe", said Claire, "its not ten minutes since you rang and asked me to come down for lunch we've not got a helicopter now have we?"

Matthew laughed, "well, I'll be waiting in the diners delight see you in a minute". Matthew put the mobile back in his pocket and Claire picked up the phone and threw it on the floor of her car deep breaths and count to ten she said to herself over and over in her head. Matthew arrived in the diners delight and took a seat to the side the ones with the tall chairs he loved those seats. He took his mobile phone from his pocket and called Claire to let her know where he was sitting so she wouldn't be looking for him when she walked in; he knew she hated walking into anywhere alone. The phone rang just as Claire was pulling into a space in the car park; she looked down at the screen she should have guessed Matthew, Claire screamed, picked up the mobile from the floor took her bag and banged the car door shut.

"Hello Matthew", said Claire.

"Hey babe", said Matthew, "I'm just letting you know that I'm sitting to the side at one of those tables with the big chairs". "I know how you hate to walk into a crowded place alone and have to find people".

"Right, right, said Claire I'm in the car park be with you in a minute". Claire walked in the door and saw Matthew straight away; she walked over and sat down across from him.

"Surprise honey", said Matthew, and handed Claire the parcel. Claire ripped the paper from the package, "ah Matthew how did you know it's just what I wanted is this an early Valentine's Day gift?"

"Not at all", said Matthew, "just a little something and don't go making plans to go out with the girls Valentines night I'm taking you out".

"Of course you are", said Claire. "What was that honey", asked Matthew?

"Oh I just said of course we are sure isn't it our anniversary". "I love you so much", said Matthew. "Yeah I know", replied Claire.

They had lunch Claire had a bottle of wine with hers so Matthew drove home. As they drove into the drive their next door neighbor Perpetual O'Brien known to all as Mrs. O'Brien was walking in home holding her grandson by the hand the eldest boy eleven years old Ciaran, she had another grandson standing on the back of the pram Cian he was six, with the littlest the baby six months old asleep in the pram.

"Jesus Claire", said Matthew "isn't she great to take that lot on at her age".

"I'm sure she's getting loads of money from the government for it and sure what else would she be doing anyways, said

Claire. Sometimes Matthew wondered at the things Claire said. Matthew parked the car and they both got out.

"Hello there, said Mrs. O'Brien, "would ye like to come in for a quick cup of coffee?" "Nah", said Claire, "we just had lunch thanks anyway".

"We'll call in for a quick chat though", said Matthew.

"Oh you go on ahead honey", said Claire, "I've got a headache coming on".

"She's just after a bottle of wine Mrs. O'Brien, said Matthew she's the worse for wear". "Ah no harm in that", said Mrs. O'Brien, "well for you we should both go for a few some day".

"Not a hope in hell thought Claire", but she smiled, and nodded as she walked in to the house. Matthew went into Mrs. O'Brien's house they had a chat and then they watched cartoons with the kids. Then their other neighbor from two doors up Shelia called up for a few minutes she didn't stay long she was rushing up home to make a fry for her nephew Seorsha who had lived with her since he was three years old. He was now thirty five and there was no need for Shelia to be rushing home on his account but Seorsha was a taxi driver and Shelia always liked to make sure he had a good meal before he went out to work for the night. Shelia hated when he was working nights at the weekend she worried that he would be robbed or assaulted or something she whished he had a different job. Matthew stayed until it was time for the kids to go to bed he read them stories and went home, he usually went to play cards on a Friday night but this Friday he and his friends were giving it a miss as the pub they usually went to was closed for renovations and they couldn't be bothered going somewhere else. Claire was lying on the couch watching sex and the city when Matthew came in home.

"Oh honey", said Matthew "I can't wait until we have a family I'd love at least three what about you?"

"Oh yeah", said Claire, "I can't wait now sush I'm watching this". Matthew sat on the couch beside Claire. "Can't you go over there sit on one of the chairs or something I was lovely and comfortable here".

"Oh", said Matthew, "I just thought we might cuddle".

"For fucks sake Matthew I told you I'm watching this".

"Okay, okay", said Matthew. The hangover's kicking in early he thought as he walked over and sat on one of the chairs poor Claire. The next day Claire had work, so had Matthew. "This is a first honey I never remember you all working a Saturday before". "It's the time of the year honey", said Claire, "we are very busy".

"Well", said Matthew, "Catriona is so nice anyways it's nice to oblige her".

"And what makes you think she's so nice", asked Claire?

Shit thought Matthew; she's going to get it out of me what am I going to do.

"Well said Matthew I never hear you complain about her so I presume she is but if you want I can ring in sick for you what's her number".

Matthew grabbed Claire's mobile phone from the bedside locker and began scrolling through the contacts. Claire dived from the bed and grabbed the phone from him.

"Jesus Christ Matthew you big child give me here my mobile how dare you go through my phone and how dare you think you can just ring my boss, just go to work will you and let me do mine".

Matthew stood pale and in shock what did I do he thought. "Honey I'm sorry I didn't mean".

"Oh Matthew", said Claire, "I'm so sorry I don't know what came over me don't mind me I didn't mean it, I think it's that bottle of wine yesterday I'm not used to the drink I'm just not myself".

Matthew smiled relieved. "It's ok babe we can't all be in good humor the whole time and wine is terrible for blowing the head of you, listen I'm away to work talk to you later I'll text you".

Matthew was a builder lately things had slowed down a bit but he knew they would be fine they had done well during the busy times. I must remember to contact the bank about that loan I applied for no point in beginning a development in the current environment Matthew thought to himself as he headed out the door. On Matthews lunch break he went to a restaurant in town Gourmet nights and booked a table for them for Valentines night. The restaurant was the nicest in town. There was a cocktail bar to the front where you could have drinks while you waited and the restaurant had the most beautiful food in town. He was friends with the owner Liam and it was he who was behind the desk and took the booking.

"See Liam", said Matthew, "I've booked us a cruise I was wondering if you could bring out the tickets with the desert".

"Yeah no bother, said Liam, you really do, do everything big don't you".

"Ah said Matthew it's our first anniversary as well and I want her to know how special she is to me".

"Yeah I remember the best wedding I was at before or since".

"Well, said Matthew I'm glad you enjoyed it".

"Yeah I did", said Liam, "don't forget to drop in those tickets before Saturday night".

"I will do", said Matthew "thanks Liam".

The days were flying by and despite Matthews's excitement he managed to say nothing. It was Friday night the night Matthew went out with his friends to play cards Billy wouldn't be able to join them tonight as he had to stay at home with his daughter as his wife was in hospital so it would just be himself Seorsha, Fionn, Kevin and Damien. "Hey babe", he had said to Claire when he came in home, "I don't have to go out we could always get a takeaway have a bottle of wine or something if you'd like".

"No, no Claire insisted you go out have a good time enjoy yourself, and don't worry about getting a taxi home I'll collect you".

I've got the best wife in town Matthew thought as he walked out the door to the pub.

He didn't like to ask Claire to drive him down after all she was going to stay up to collect him; he didn't want to take advantage.

"So", said Fionn, "tell us what your plans for Valentines are Matthew".

"I'm taking Claire on a cruise for two weeks".

"Do you not think that you might be over doing it a bit like you won't be able to keep this up, said Seorsha?"

"Sure she deserves it what would I do without her?" Matthew said.

"You'd be a lot better off for one thing", said Damien laughing, "so are we going to play cards or what?"

They played cards and soon the bar staff were calling last orders. Half one and Matthew stood outside waiting for Claire he didn't want to ring and rush her he knew she would soon be there she wouldn't forget him. Two am Matthew was still standing waiting for Claire he didn't want to start walking as he didn't know which way Claire would come and he didn't want her to have to drive around looking for him like a fool. It was cold out and Matthew began to shiver he was starting to worry what if something had happened to Claire. He took out his mobile phone and rang her; the phone rang and rang but no answer. Matthew began to walk home worried sick he started to run sweating exhausted he arrived at the front door he opened the door and ran in. There was Claire in front of the television watching a dvd.

"Oh your home", said Claire, "is it that time already, I didn't realize".

"Thank God", said Matthew, "I was worried sick I thought something happened you". "Don't be daft", said Claire; "I'm trying to watch the end of this sush".

"Okay honey", said Matthew and put his arm around Claire.

"Phew you stink", said Claire.

"I'm going to head up to bed see you in the morning", said Matthew laughing.

The phone ringing the following morning woke Matthew he felt like he had just fallen asleep, Claire was shaking him answer that will you babe? Matthew yawned and stretched.

"Hello?" "Hello this is Justine from the travel agents I'm just ringing to let you know that those tickets are here for you whenever you're ready to collect them".

"Oh thanks, thanks", said Matthew, he jumped out of bed and took the phone downstairs.

Thank God he thought that Claire didn't answer the phone.

"You start early I'd have slept on it only for you".

"Ah not really, said Justine".

"Well thanks I'll be in and collect the tickets on the way to work", said Matthew. "Right", said Justine, "they'll be here for you, remember them now you leave Sunday, and we close at one today happy valentines day bye for now".

"Talk to you", said Matthew.

"Who was that", Claire asked, when Matthew returned to the bedroom.

"No one", Matthew replied.

"Sounded like a girls voice to me", said Claire.

"Yeah babe", said Matthew, leaning over Claire lying in the bed and giving her a kiss on the lips Claire put her arms around his neck, "its just some woman wants me to do some building for her that's all you jealous?"

"Na not a bit", said Claire, "sure who apart from me would have you?"

Matthew laughed and Claire pulled him down onto the bed. "Ah babe", said Matthew, "I have to get up and go to work".

"Its Saturday you fool" said Claire.

"Yeah I know", said Matthew. "Ring in sick", said Claire, "go on ring the lads and tell them you won't be in".

"I'd love to", said Matthew, "but I can't". It was on the tip of his tongue to say because I'm going to be missing for two weeks from Monday he just stopped himself in time. "You're a workaholic you are you know that; go on so fuck off with yourself".

Matthew reached down from the bed and pulled his wallet from his jeans which were lying on the floor where he had left them the night before. " Never mind babe I'll be home in a few hours why don't you ring the girls go do something nice for yourself for the day". "I paid the credit cards for the month there two weeks ago I used one of them don't ask me which but there's still credit on it", Matthew handed Claire his little wallet with all the credit and bank cards in it.

"I don't need that said Claire". "Go on", said Matthew, "take it and treat yourself, I feel really bad leaving you". Claire smiled, "and so you should any good husband would ring in sick when his wife tells him to especially on Valentines Day".

"Is that so", said Matthew, "and tell me this what would a good husband do when it was time to pay the bills?"

Claire laughed, Matthew got into the shower dressed and left. Claire turned over in the bed and went back to sleep. Matthew didn't want anything to go wrong the first thing he did was go to Travel's for the tickets before he went in he bought a box of Roses to give the girls behind the counter. The whole shop was draped in red. The white candles in the grate had been replaced with red ones. Red balloons in the shape of love hearts hung in clusters of about twelve around the room. There were little baskets with sweets in the shape of love hearts wrapped in red paper on the end tables beside the sofas and also on the counter. Justine wasn't there a girl called Amanda was behind the counter.

"Hi I'm Matthew Ryan", said Matthew, "I'm here to collect tickets", Justine called me earlier.

"Oh so you're the guy who's bought the most expensive Valentines gift in town", said Amanda, "so tell me this how does a girl land a guy like you, where do ye hang out?" she asked as she went over to a filing cabinet and pulled out the envelope with Matthew's name on it. Matthew could feel his ears start to turn red and then yeah he could feel his face burn.

"Well that's me sorted", said Matthew, "thanks for your help here's a few sweets for ye happy Valentines Day". Matthew got in the car and went straight to the restaurant to give Liam the tickets. Liam wasn't there but the waitress promised him faithfully nothing would happen the tickets she would guard them with her life until Liam came in.

"Thanks, thanks said Matthew he'll know what it's all about, he'll know what to do with them". Matthew then headed for the site where they were working he was the only one there, he gave the place a quick once over before getting in the car with a big sigh of joy that was the last he'd see of dust for a fortnight sea and sun from tomorrow out life was sweet. Matthew drove to the barbers and got his hair done and a wet shave. Matthews's hair was a dirty blonde he had light blonde highlights through it that made his blue eyes look bluer. He was constantly tanned from working on the buildings.

"You should do modeling", said the girl who washed his hair for him. "What do you say Emmet?" she shouted over to her co worker?

"Yeah ,yeah" , replied Emmet, "you know what my darling niece is at don't you she's looking for models for the charity fashion show the transition years are organizing for St. Vincent de Paul".

Matthew kept looking at the girl she reminded him of someone, or they had met somewhere or something he just couldn't place her. Well said Matthew that's a great thing to do especial at the moment the way things are going more and more people are going to need them.

"So", said Yvonne, "will you do it, we're having a mock wedding you'd be perfect as the groom".

"I'd love to", said Matthew, "but I'm off on a cruise Sunday for two weeks".

"Oh my God", said Yvonne, "its you, your grand the shows not for three months yet, the end of May". "We're having a choreographer and everything a dj and all, it will be great".

"I'm sure it will", said Matthew, "what did you mean before it's me?"

"You're the guy who is taking his wife on a surprise cruise, Justine is my mam I met you the other day in the shop".

"Oh yeah", said Matthew, "I knew your face was familiar".

"Well mam is giving Tony a terrible time of it reckon he will have to take her on a holiday soon or it will be curtains, hope you realize what you've started", they all laughed.

"So Yvonne tell me this what age are you?" "Almost fifteen I work here with Emmet Saturday and holidays and I'm going to go fulltime and on the books and all amn't I Emmet once I'm sixteen".

"We will see how it goes", Emmet replied.

"So basically, said Matthew you should be paying me for letting you near my hair". "Why did you not think I washed it right?"

"I'm only messing with you Yvonne your great; they should bottle you and sell you for a tonic".

"Yeah your wife's the luckiest woman alive", Yvonne said, returning to their original topic, "look at you she's got the whole package". Matthew could feel himself burning up. "Ah and modest too", said Yvonne, "look at him Emmet his burning up".

"Ah bless", said Emmet, thinking why any of the good ones can't be gay? "His all yours now", said Yvonne, "that's me done for".

Would you like to take a seat over here Matthew? "Yvonne", said Emmet, "are you not going to offer Matthew a cup of coffee??"

"Matthew will you have a cup of coffee", said Yvonne, "the kettle is in the back there and the coffee is beside it, so is the sugar and the milk is in the fridge I'll take mine black".

"Yvonne", roared Emmet Yvonne and Matthew laughed. Emmet got ready to shave Matthew.

"You've got your work cut out for you there", Matthew said to Emmet.

"Sure", said Emmet, "I have to admit I look forward to Saturdays she's brought life into the place into me". "The best thing I ever did was to move back down here and get to know my family again". "Yvonne's my niece Matthew, but I'm really only getting to know her in the past year". "So", said Emmet, "are you all packed?"

"Not at all", said Matthew, "we're going out for dinner to-night I've got reservations for seven we're not leaving until two tomorrow, there is loads of time to pack besides Claire is better at packing than me I wouldn't know what to pack I'd bring all the wrong stuff".

"It's a great time of the year for getting away too", said Emmet, "lifts the spirits the sunshine".

"Yeah", said Matthew, "I won't miss the weather here that's for sure". Yvonne returned and handed Matthew a cup of coffee.

"And tell me this", said Emmet, "where is that tan from?"

"The buildings", said Matthew, "it isn't so much a tan as the weathered look".

Emmet laughed, "well it does it for me".

"Right Yvonne I'm all done you can sweep up here when you're ready". Yvonne put down her magazine and went back to working as Emmet styled Matthews hair.

"So you're getting yourself all spruced up for the holiday what about your wife if she knows nothing about it maybe she'd like to get her hair and nails and all done before she goes away", said Yvonne joking.

"That's a fair point", said Matthew. He took out his mobile and rang Claire the phone rang and rang but there was no answer so he left a voice message. Hey babes it's me I was just thinking why don't you go get your hair and nails done its Valentines day you deserve it don't forget we're going out for dinner love you. Yvonne turned to Emmet while Matthew was leaving his message on the phone and stuck her fingers down her throat.

"Now", said Emmet, jealousy isn't an admirable quality in a lady is it Matthew?". Matthew laughed.

"Well", said Yvonne, no offence to you but see that jammy wife of yours she's nothing only a bitch you could do so much better and you can tell her I said that to".

"Well", said Matthew, "that's your opinion you're entitled to it and I'm delighted for you that you're so perfect that you can pass judgment on others, are you finished with my hair?

"Yeah, yeah don't mind her", said Emmet; "it's that time of the month". "Apologies" Emmet mouthed to Yvonne.

"No", Yvonne mouthed back.

"Oh you better if you know what's good for you", said Emmet.

"I'm right", said Yvonne.

"APOLOGIES", said Emmet, and took his mobile from his pocket to call Justine. "I'll call your mammy".

"I'm sorry Matthew I didn't mean to offend you", said Yvonne.

Matthew took his coat from the hanger took out his wallet and slammed money down on the counter. "Best of luck to ye", said Matthew, and walked out the door.

"See you"; said Emmet, "do you like your job here?"

"Yeah I love it", said Yvonne.

"Well unless you want to loose it you better keep your opinion to your self in future". "Yeah whatever you'll all see yet I'll be proved right".

"Tell me more", said Emmet.

"I thought you wanted me to keep my opinion to myself", said Yvonne.

"Only in front of the customers love tell me more I'll but on the kettle".

Yvonne turned the open sign to closed and went over and sat down waiting for her tea. "So", said Emmet, returning with two cups of tea. Yvonne took a packet of cigarettes from her pocket.

"Not in here you don't", said Emmet and at your age in this day and age I'm amazed that anyone would sell them to you.

"Whatever", said Yvonne.

"So tell me what you know".

"I was up in the accountants office there a few Fridays ago asking if we did this fashion show thing would they be interested in having advertising space in the broucher". "I was in the office when Claire got flowers from Matthew she was such a bitch saying he wrecked her head". "She gets loads of flowers and sweets and stuff at work from him". "She either gives away the flowers or throws them in the bin I swear down I heard it all". "Then there I was on Monday I went down to me mam at lunch for me dinner to the shop ya know and in comes the man himself Matthew to book a cruise for her". "He must be thick as a ditch he must be a male bimbo.

"Ah said Emmet aren't we all fools in love?"

2

Claire paced over and back across the floor clutching the cup of coffee that she held in her hands as much for the comfort of its warmth as its taste. Her breathing was fast and shallow she felt as though all life was being squeezed out of her. She had that terrible foreboding feeling in the pit of her stomach, she had that a lot lately she felt like the walls were closing in on her, her darkest imaginings engulfed her. She muttered to herself while she paced.

Why does everything bore me what's wrong with me, I want for nothing yet Matthew bores me, work bores me the only time I feel alive is when…

Her mobile rang distracting her from her thoughts and making her jump she looked at the screen of her mobile and a scream erupted from deep within her. Matthew.

She threw the phone to the floor and let it go to voice mail. When the phone beeped to tell her there was a message she dialed 171 and listened. Claire hung up and the phone rang again she jumped looked at the phone and smiled. "Hello Dave", Claire answered and all her worries left her. "Hey babe Dave replied are you alone?"

"Yeah", replied Claire, "Matthew went to work he just left a voice message on the phone for me to get my hair done or that what you at?"

"I was going to come over to you", said Dave, "I was thinking of closing up the shop early".

"Oh", said Claire, "that would be great, I feel so I don't know what I'd love to see you, but no I'd better go get my hair done we are probably going out for a meal or something tonight its valentines and our anniversary remember". "

Ah, said Dave I haven't seen you since we went away for the day last Saturday, I'll only call over for a few minutes. Of course if you don't want to see me?" "

No, no of course I want to see you, you know that it's just I don't want to hurt Matthew he'd do anything for me he deserves better, sure if its only for a few minutes. "I'll be there in fifteen minutes", said Dave.

Claire hung up the phone and turned to go upstairs to check her hair and make up as she put her foot on the first step the door bell rang. She recognized the shape in the door it was Mrs. O'Brien.

What does she want now thought Claire as she opened the door.

"Hello there Mrs. O'Brien how are you?" Claire asked as she answered the door.

"I'm grand thanks Claire I was just wondering if I could ask you a favor?" Claire sighed heavily she was all in favor of community spirit so long as she was the one benefiting from it.

Mrs. O'Brien pushed on, "himself was in last night and he said that if there was anything either of you could do to help just to give a shout, sure he is the best in the world the kids love him he read them a story last night and all".

"I'm sure he did, said Claire, the sarcasm in her voice undisguised".

"Well", said Mrs. O'Brien, "like I just said Matthew said if I needed anything to give you a shout, and you see Hanna here has been sick and I have to go to the shop for potatoes for the dinner for the little ones before they come back from soccer, and I don't want to take her out in the cold". "I was wondering if you could take her for me I'll be an hour at the outside probably only thirty minutes and she's fast asleep in the pram I've just changed her and she's had a bottle so I doubt she'll wake up before I'm back". "What", said Claire? "I don't think so". "Oh", said Mrs. O'Brien taken aback, "oh well I see you are busy sorry to have bothered you I'll leave you to it".

"Bye now", said Claire, "take care".

Mrs. O'Brien walked away from the door pushing the pram she was exhausted, she wouldn't have it any other way but it wasn't easy having all these children at her age. After her chat with Claire she felt drained why had she ever thought to ask her she felt stupid and upset.

"Hello there", Sheila called over her wall she was out weeding the daffodils.

"Shelia how are you?" replied Mrs. O'Brien.

"Not a bother on me replied Shelia come up for a cup of coffee".

"I can't," said Mrs. O'Brien I've got to go get potatoes for the dinner".

"Don't worry about that", said Shelia, "let ye come in out of the cold I've the kettle on and it will only take a minute and I've a big bag of potatoes that we'll never get through before they are gone off".

"Are you sure that would be great if your certain", said Mrs. O'Brien, "your ones just taken the wind out of me". "

Course I am", replied Shelia, "let ye come in out of the cold I don't know why you would ask that stuck up cow for anything anyway". "I heard how she talked to you at the door I was behind the wall weeding I wouldn't trust her with Hanna to begin with". Claire was back inside pacing she forgot about checking her hair and make up.

Why couldn't I have just taken the little one for an hour she was asleep and all I'll be blackened now to all of them she thought away to herself

She looked up the window was open.

Shit, shit thought Claire did I just say that out loud.

Something caught her attention from the side of her eye it was Dave pulling into the drive. Claire opened the door and once Dave was inside she jumped into his arms, he carried her to the sofa and within seconds they were naked oblivious to the time that had elapsed.

After Matthew left the barbers he walked around town thinking he had an uneasy feeling in the pit of his stomach.

This is daft he thought why do I feel uneasy because of some stupid remark from a teenager, *but what did she mean, how would she know Claire? I'm daft thought Matthew I'm looking for problems where there are none.*

He put it out of his mind and headed for the car park to get his car. Matthew got in his car and drove home the traffic ahead of him annoyed him, he had no patience to sit in traffic, he was to excited he just wanted to get home and start his Valentines Day. Claire will be surprised to see me home at four o clock in the day I can't wait to see the look on her face when she sees the tickets. Matthew couldn't help but smile away to himself as he drove home. Matthew decided to take the slip road onto the bypass to try to avoid the traffic, but he got caught in traffic anyway and ended up sitting in the car daydreaming.

Nice house, nice neighbors a wife who is my soul mate, a best friend I've known a life time I must be the luckiest man in the world I have a fairytale life.

Matthew drove into the estate Mrs. O'Brien and Shelia were heading up the path towards him Matthew rolled down the window. "

Well ladies what's the story are we winning?"

"Ah", said Shelia, "no news with us alls quiet we're just out for a walk with the children".

"Yeah", said Mrs. O'Brien, "and then Shelia's just heading down to mine for a game of cards". "

Oh that's nice", said Matthew, "myself and Claire are away out tonight for dinner".

"Oh right", said Mrs. O'Brien, "well enjoy your night".

"Thanks said Matthew we are going on two weeks holidays from Sunday so we will see you both when we get back". "Claire doesn't know anything about it I'm going to tell her tonight over dinner".

"She's a lucky woman", said Mrs. O'Brien.

"Yeah", said Shelia, both women exchanged a look, "I hope she appreciates you". Matthew laughed, "well ladies I got to love ye and leave ye enjoy your evening".

As Matthew drew up to their line of houses he spotted Dave's car. Matthew was delighted it was perfect his best friend and the best man from his wedding was there to celebrate their first anniversary with them.

He remembered thought Matthew as he pulled into the drive.

He pulled up the hand brake turned off the engine took out his mobile and rang the restaurant to change his reservation for two to one for three he wanted to do it before he went in home just incase there was a problem with having an extra person. He didn't want to be inviting Dave only to disappoint him. That done he locked the car pulled the keys out of his jacket pocket and turned the key in the door. It was then it happened the fairytale like a house of cards caught in the draft from the door collapsed around him. On the couch that he had paid two thousand euros for his best friend and wife on their anniversary lay naked.

"Fuck, fuck" shouted Claire wrapping the throw from the couch around her. "Matthew your home early". "It wasn't meant to happen like this".

"Big man, big man," said Dave, as he walked naked towards Matthew. "I'm so sorry the last thing I wanted to do was hurt you".

Matthew stood numb he couldn't breath there was a stabbing pain in his chest this was the greatest rush of emotion he had ever felt, he began to walk backwards from the scene as though in an attempt to rewind what his eyes had seen and mind couldn't comprehend he stood there in the hall, the door open behind him without the will to move.

"We never wanted it to happen this way", said Claire, "but now that it's happened and it had to happen sooner or later you might as well know we are in love". "We are as much victims in all this as you Matthew we did our best to fight it but this is something stronger than either of us". "Matthew you know I still love you but I'm just not in love with you".

"Matthew", said Dave, "we hope some day you can forgive us and we can all be friends".

Matthew ignored Dave and grabbed Claire by both hands, "please honey tell me what I can do to fix this anything, anything you just name it".

Claire sighed heavily "that's just it, you can't fix it I can't do this anymore your constant need for validation, your ringing me a thousand times a day, the constant texts, the flowers the gifts you suffocated me". "Jesus Matthew you're so needy, so weak even now when you should be fighting for me you stand there a miserable pathetic lump".

Still undressed and wrapped in the throw from the couch Claire turned to Dave. "Come on love".

Dave took a tea towel from the floor and wrapped it around his waist not being long enough the tea towel gaped at the back exposing most of his arse as he swaggered out the door after Claire who called back over her shoulder. "

I'll call tomorrow for my clothes and stuff pass me my bag will you Dave incase I need the credit cards or that".

Dave walked towards the chair where the bag sat picked it up and handed it with all their cards to Claire. Matthew felt strange it was like he was watching the whole thing happen to someone else and he was shouting to him you fool ask for your cards back, ask for your cards back.

This must be an out of body experience, Matthew thought to himself as he watched as Dave picked up the bag and walked towards Claire who snatched it from his hand and sailed out the door.

"Jesus Mary and holy Saint Joseph", Mrs. O'Brien shouted loudly as she saw the pair emerge from the house. "Shelia something is really wrong next door poor Matthew would you look at the state of the pair of them".

Just then Dave turned around. "Jesus, Jesus Shelia would you look at me mans arse if it wasn't for poor Matthew this would be hilarious". "Jesus, said Shelia this is priceless it's better than television there is never anything on that".

"Should we go in check on Matthew?" Mrs. O'Brien asked.

"Ah no", said Shelia, "I'd say he wants some privacy now tomorrow evening we'll go in see what we can do, but now I'd say the last thing he wants is company".

"Your right", said Mrs. O'Brien. "He probably wants to be alone".

And so it was reality hit home with the subtlety of a bull in a china shop, and Matthew stood back helpless as the love of his life turned and walked out the door with his best friend. He was rooted to the spot not realizing that the front door lay wide open, that daylight had faded into night and not just that evening darkness but the two in the morning black, black night. Three am, four am, five am and Matthew still stood there with the cold night air blowing through him. He was engulfed in a daze of disbelief, to move was to leave the moment when Claire was there. His body defied him his feet rooted to the time the time before Claire walked out the door, he could not step forward into the uncertainty of the now that was unfolding before him a now totally out of his control.

I'm dreaming that's what it is I'm asleep it's Friday night not Saturday I'm just in home from the pub and I'm in bed asleep and the drink and the fright I got and the running home has given me nightmares that's all, Matthew thought to himself.

His mind raced rewinding and fast forwarding the day if only he hadn't come home so early, if only he'd noticed something was wrong maybe it wouldn't have come to this. Night had faded its stark darkness softened to the amber glow of dawn, birds were singing and the street sweeping truck hummed as it made its way around the estate Matthew was still unmoved. It was seven am people were up and moving though not in great numbers as it was Sunday the one day of the week that allowed for a lie in for the majority of the estate. Mrs. Perpetual O'Brien was up making a morning bottle for Hanna. She walked over to the kitchen press to get out the cereal and left it on the table for the little boys, mind you she thought it could be closer to twelve when they get up they are starting to lie in a lot lately since they went back to school after Christmas. It was then she noticed it, she pulled the mobile from her pocket and phoned Shelia.

"Jesus Shelia there's something seriously wrong Matthews's door is still open they never did anything to him?"

"Jesus Perpetual I don't know should we call the guards?"

"And what if there's nothing wrong we'll look like two daft auld ones. I'll tell you what Perpetual we'll meet at the gate in a sec and go in and see if everything is ok maybe there is no one there at all".

"Fine I'll just check the kids and meet you out front".

Mrs. O'Brien went up stairs; she checked the boy's room they were both sleeping. Next she peeped into her own room where she had Hanna's cot. She was asleep also so she flicked on the baby monitor took the receiver from the mantle piece in the sitting room and headed to her next door neighbors gate. "What's that", asked Shelia pointing to the baby monitor, "walkie talkies". "

This is no time to be joking", said Mrs. O'Brien.

"I know", said Shelia, "come on and we'll see what the story is".

They walked in the open gate up to the open door and Shelia being the first to notice she nudged Mrs. O'Brien who looked up and they both took a sigh of relief there before them stood Matthew his back facing them. Mrs. O'Brien turned to walk away and Shelia followed her.

Shelia turned to Mrs. O'Brien and said, "so what are we going to do?"

"I'm going to go in home rouse the children and get them their breakfasts then we are going to go in there and get Matthew sorted he is in shock but with the help of god he'll have shifted himself by the time we go back in there I'll be twenty minutes I'll grab Hanna put her in the pram and tell the boys once they eat their cereal to head straight into us".

"Right", said Shelia "I'll spread the word of what's happened the more people around him now the better it will get him over the hump"

3

Twenty minutes later Mrs. O'Brien and Shelia re entered the house. Mrs. O'Brien walked up to Matthew and put her arm around him. He was still unmoved she had expected him to move but he didn't he remained rooted to the spot though he turned his head slightly to look at her. Tears welled up in his eyes.

"She's left me she's gone" and Matthew burst out crying.

"Come on love", said Mrs. O'Brien, "you can't spend the rest of your life standing there". "Your frozen come on and well get something hot into you". "

I'll put the kettle on", said Shelia.

Matthew followed Shelia into the kitchen like a lost lamb. Mrs. O'Brien turned and pushed the pram in front of her into the kitchen.

"Matthew", said Shelia, "have you an electric blanket in your bedroom if you like I'll go up and turn it on for you while the kettle is boiling".

"I have", said Matthew.

"I'll run up Shelia while your making the tea", said Mrs. O'Brien, "that's the best thing for you right now Matthew a bit of grub and a good sleep, nothing in this world seems as bad when your looking at it after a good sleep".

Mrs. O'Brien went up and turned on the electric blanket.

"Shelia", asked Matthew, is Seorsha home?

"Yeah", said Shelia, "I'll ring him".

"Ah no leave him have his lie in but maybe this evening if he is not busy he might call down", said Matthew.

"I'm sure he would", said Shelia, "he is off all day he'd be glad to".

Hanna dropped her bottle from her hand and couldn't reach it and began to cry Matthew went over and picked her up out of the pram and walked around the kitchen with her he went over to the press with all the pots in it and took out a saucepan he went to the drawer and took out a wooden spoon he but them both on the floor and sat Hanna down beside them. Hanna began banging the wooden spoon of the saucepan. Upstairs Mrs. O'Brien heard the racket first Hanna crying and then the banging she came rushing down the stairs and into the kitchen and burst out laughing.

"I thought something fell on her, was it you gave her that Matthew?"

"Yeah", said Matthew, "I hope you don't mind I took her out of the pram she was getting bored in there".

"No at all", said Mrs. O'Brien, "you're a natural".

"Where are the other two", said Matthew? "

"Out home finishing their cereal", said Mrs. O'Brien, "I had better go check on them". "Sure you head home altogether", said Shelia; "I'll stay here till Matthew goes up to have a sleep".

"If you're sure", said Mrs. O'Brien.

"I won't go to bed now", said Matthew, "I don't want to be up all night Mrs. O'Brien why don't you bring them in here I don't fancy being alone right now if it's ok with you".

"For a bit so", said Mrs. O'Brien, "but as soon as you have enough of them say the word".

Mrs. O'Brien went out and grabbed the two boys and brought them into Matthews along with a package of rashers and a dozen eggs while Matthew played with the children Mrs. O'Brien and Shelia made toast and fried eggs and rashers. There was a knock at the door Matthew jumped up hopefully expecting it to be Claire. That it was only a big mistake and everything was going to be ok, but it was Seorsha and even though Matthew was glad to see him, his face fell with disappointment.

"I smelt the fry and thought this would be where ye would be", said Seorsha.

"Come in, said Matthew, have you heard?"

"Yeah", said Seorsha, "I have".

And Matthew began to cry. Seorsha but his arm around him and the two men went into the sitting room. Matthew stayed up until nine o clock that Sunday night and Seorsha, Shelia,

Perpetual and the children stayed with him all day. Matthew spent the day intermittently crying but he never spoke of what had happened it was as if he thought that talking about it acknowledging it would make it real.

"Should we mention it to him", said Shelia to Mrs. O'Brien at one stage, "like he has things to do to get himself sorted".

"Ah no", said Mrs. O'Brien, "he's in shock at the minute in denial and he's had no sleep, besides there isn't much he can do today, tomorrow we'll tackle it the main thing is to make sure he does nothing stupid".

"Yeah your right", said Shelia, "she was his world he adored her, it might be no harm if Seorsha stayed here tonight so he won't be alone".

Matthew sat on the sofa watching Seorsha wrestling with the two little boys. It's all going to be ok he told himself, Claire will be back tomorrow she would probably have been back today only she doesn't know what to say to me but it will all be ok, she'll be back tomorrow. It's all Dave's fault Claire would never do anything like this. I'll make things better when she comes back make a fuss of her. Everything will be okay this is just a little hiccup. Jesus I don't fancy being on my own tonight, I wonder would it be too much to ask Seorsha to stay. Shelia and Mrs. O'Brien were out in the hall talking Matthew was distracted from his thoughts by them calling Seorsha out to them. Seorsha came back in.

"Matthew" he said, "would you like to have a few cans a hand or two of cards, and sure if it was ok with you I'd crash here with you for the night".

"Oh", said Matthew, "that would be great I wanted to ask you but I didn't want to bother you, I don't fancy being alone but I'm sure this will all have passed by tomorrow and Claire will be back".

Mrs. O'Brien and Shelia stood in the doorway Seorsha looked towards them and they exchanged looks something told them it would be a long time if ever Claire walked through the door again. They spent the rest of the evening playing cards. Shelia had dressed the bed in the spare room across from Matthews for Seorsha.

"Seorsha", said Mrs. O'Brien, "watch him like a hawk leave the door open if your worried call us he's not good at all". "

Don't worry", said Seorsha, "he'll be fine, I'll keep a good eye on him, we all will this is a long time coming you know, it's not today or yesterday that Claire started sleeping with Dave ".

"No", said Mrs. O'Brien "I didn't have a clue".

At nine o clock when exhaustion finally over took Matthew he went up to his bed that was roasting thanks to Mrs. O'Brien turning on the blanket hours before, Mrs. O'Brien took the children home, they were exhausted from all the playing and fell straight asleep. Mrs. O'Brien made lunches for the next day at school and ironed and hung up uniforms. Shelia went home and put a few bits and pieces together for Seorsha for the night and took them up to him.

"You're a great nephew Seorsha I'd be lost without you," said Shelia.

"Would you stop", said Seorsha, "sure what would I do without you?"

By half ten they were all asleep even Matthew who had passed the day in a daze it had all felt surreal to him.

I'll wake up tomorrow and everything will be okay, he thought, everything will be normal again.

It was Monday morning Seorsha woke at seven he was always busy Monday morning driving kids to school and people to work. There wasn't a move on Matthew; Seorsha went up to his room to check on him twice finally at ten to eight Seorsha went home to get his car. He had gotten two jobs already. Shelia was at the door waiting for him.

"So how did it go?? Have you had any breakfast?"

"He's gutted", Aunty Shelia, "we'll have to keep a good eye on him for a while; no I've no appetite I'll get something around eleven".

"Right so pet I'm going to head up to Perpetual drive safely we will see you later once the kids are sorted for school the two of us will head into him. Thanks for last night pet".

Shelia headed up to Mrs. O'Brien and Seorsha headed off to work. There was not a dog in the ditch who didn't know what had happened between Matthew and Claire. Matthew woke up at nine o'clock wondering where the voices he could hear were coming from. Then he could get the smell of cooking. Then he heard a baby laughing he wrapped a dressing gown around him and went down stairs.

What would I do without the neighbors thought Matthew at least this nightmare will be over by the end of the week Claire will be back and I will never talk to that Dave again as long as I live.

"Good man yourself", said Mrs. O'Brien, "you're up". "You should have stayed in bed", said Shelia, "we were going to bring the breakfast up to you".

"Ah", said Matthew, "its too late now I'm up".

Hanna was crawling around the floor.

"Come up here to me missus, said Matthew, will we turn on Peppa pig and see what she's doing?"

"How are you doing Matthew?" asked Mrs. O'Brien.

"Ah", said Matthew, "I'll be fine I know when Claire comes back we will have a lot to talk about, but it's only a glitch and we all have them".

Just then the doorbell rang word was out Catriona, Ashley and Adrian were at the door Tom was locking the car and heading towards the house. Matthew was shocked to see Yvonne amongst this group that was so much older than her. Matthew had to admit he liked the attention. Mrs. O'Brien, Shelia, Maria the polish lady who lived across the street and Anna the Russian lady who lived beside her made tea and coffee and dished out biscuits to all and sundry.

"God help us", Mrs. O'Brien was saying out in the kitchen, "he was standing there all night like a fool with the door open".

"Yeah", said Shelia, "he was in total shock literally rooted to the floor".

"And she seemed so quiet", said Mrs. O'Brien.

"Well", said Shelia, "it's the quiet ones you've got to watch the auld bitch, harlot".

"Yes", said Anna, "she is what you would say a whore".

"No, no said Maria she is not a whore, a whore is paid she was not paid no Mrs. O'Brien?"

" No, no, said Mrs. O'Brien not paid but still a whore".

"So what are we going to do with him, asked Shelia?"

"I don't know, said Mrs. O'Brien I really don't know".

Down at the building site where Matthew had been working word had filtered through to Kevin, Fionn and Damien. Billy had told them he had heard from his friend Nora when he went out to get milk for their morning coffee on the site, who had heard from her next door neighbor Sally who was friends with Maria the polish neighbor of Claire and Matthew.

"Jesus", said Damien, "I wonder did she tell him before or after the meal".

"By all accounts", said Billy, "he found them at it".

"Do we know who it was? Fionn asked".

"It was that best man fellow from the wedding Dave".

"Do ye know what", said Kevin; "I couldn't take to him that day no matter how hard I tried".

"You know", said Billy, "it could have been going on even then it's only a year ago". "Yeah, said Damien, exactly a year what kind of person does that to some one on their anniversary, and to think he treated her like gold dust".

"Come on", said Billy, "we'll close up shop here and head up there".

They all piled into the van and drove down to the house. As they walked in the open door the smell of household cleaner mixed with that of frying greeted them as an army of women dusted cleaned and cooked.

"What times are ye back to work", asked Mrs. O'Brien?

"There's no more work for us today", said Fionn. "We're needed here more today". "Fare play to ye", said Mrs. O'Brien.

"I'll put on more fry, said Shelia".

"So said Fionn how did ye hear?"

Mrs. O'Brien told the tale of poorly clad arses and naked woman wrapped in sofa throws clutching her handbag finishing by saying the auld slapper the trollop and the poor creator sure he was stood there in that spot overnight unable to move he was in such shock. Mrs. O'Brien gestured to the spot with a nod of her head. Anyone could have walked in on top of him. "

He's lucky to have such good neighbors", said Fionn.

"Sure we do our best", said Mrs. O'Brien.

Matthew had fallen into silence for the best part of an hour but with so much coming and going no one noticed. Billy walked over to him.

"Had ye been out to dinner mate I don't like to bring this up but where are the tickets you should maybe see about getting some of your money back".

"They are still down in the restaurant, said Matthew, we never left the house happy fucking anniversary", and with this Matthew burst into uncontrollable sobs, "and we were so happy". "She loves me you know it's Dave he turned her head she's so innocent and quiet".

"For Christ's sake man would you catch yourself on, said Kevin, she's nothing but a bitch we all thought you were too good for her your well rid".

Fionn walked in the front door he had been on his mobile phone to Liam in the restaurant about Matthews's tickets. "Liam was wondering what happened to you Saturday night. He's on the way over here with the tickets and then the two of us will head down to the travel agents to see if we can get your money back".

Just then Claire without knocking sailed in the door not a bother on her. She was wearing a mans rugby shirt and track suit bottoms yet it had to be acknowledged she still looked good. I'm here for my clothes and stuff.

"I'm staying at Dave's, look at the state of you, you haven't shaved or anything". Claire sniffed the air around Matthew "you stink". "I suppose you've been sitting there since Saturday night feeling sorry for yourself".

Mrs. O'Brien could take no more and ran at Claire with the sweeping brush. "Get out of here you whore ya". "You'll get no clothes here today talking to the poor man like that and him without a bad word to say about you after what you did".

Claire stared straight at Mrs. O'Brien to determine if she was holding the brush as a prop or if it was possible that the brush might become a deadly weapon. Not certain and thinking it unwise to try her luck Claire retreated from the house as a great cheer rose for Mrs. O'Brien from all present.

I never liked any of those neighbors anyways thought Claire as she left the house screw the lot of them I'm well rid.

There was a light tap on the open door and they all turned around to look there stood Liam. Come in cried Mrs. O'Brien now recognized by one and all as chief cook and bottle washer.

Liam walked straight over to Matthew and extended his hand and said with a sincerity fitting a wake. "I'm sorry for your trouble that all bad luck may go with her".

"Sure we never had a day's bad luck", said Matthew, "and he began to sob again".

Liam didn't know where to luck or what to say so he turned to Fionn. "Will we go see if we can get some of this money back or what?"

"Grand said Fionn come on and we'll head".

4

Justine sat in the waiting area of the bank.

"Oliver will be with you shortly", called over the girl from the customer service desk. The story Melanie, Jane and Amanda told her at their morning break was still turning over in her mind.

It's amazing, so sad she thought and he seemed such a nice guy, imagine to go to all that trouble to find out that your wife was cheating on you with your best friend. Who needs soaps in this town?

It had been a very bad year for holidays and the end of 2008 hadn't been great either, Justine put that down to oil prices. I'll have some talking to do to get this overdraft extended. If only I could think of some way to boost sales, to attract customers. Even the great reductions in air fares this year didn't seem to bring the people in. She already knew she was very competitive she just needed to get people through the door.

Right Justine, Oliver walked towards her, his hand extended.

"We'll head down this way to my office for a chat".

Once inside the windowless box sized room Oliver sat behind the desk and Justine sat facing him. "

I'm afraid Justine", said Oliver, "it's not looking good". "How many people have you working down there with you?"

"Three", Justine replied.

"Well said Oliver the first thing we have to look at is the possibility of you cutting back on the staff and then maybe get together a proposal on ideas to get more punters through the door".

"No", said Justine, "I couldn't do that". "I couldn't possibly let anyone go we've all been friends long before this shop". "We know one another for a lifetime I can't let anyone go".

Oliver continued as if he never heard Justine, "push the winter sun and all that, as it stands I'm afraid it would be impossible for us to extend your overdraft any further". "But", said Justine, "it's only for the short term only to tide me over until things pick up".

"If", said Oliver, "you can show us that this is a viable business then we will be able to help you". "But", Oliver continued, "to be quiet frank with you we would be doing you no favors helping you into more debt if it was a case of throwing good money after bad". "Sit down brain storm come up with ideas show us the possibilities prove this business is viable, show us the figures and like I said we will see what we can do for you". "But as things stand I'm afraid I may as well be straight with you first as last, this business is unviable". "We will make another appointment for four weeks time and we can sit down and you can show us what you've come up with and we'll go from there". Justine stood up to leave Oliver extended his hand she shook it deflated her stomach felt sick. Justine headed back to the travel agents to share the bad news with her friends. If there was only some way she could get some publicity for her shop, even if she could in some way diversify. She didn't want to loose her business or her staff. They weren't her staff they were her friends.

Maybe this is one of the reasons they say you should never go into business with your friends, Justine thought.

She felt as though it was her fault the business was failing and by extension her fault that her friend's future employment was uncertain.

Fionn and Liam sat in Liam's grey Lexis and looked at each other.

"Well", said Liam, who could have seen that coming.

"Ah, said Fionn, he was blinded to her faults any fool could see what she was after, and he's still in there defending her".

"He's so soft, said Liam; do you think he'll get through it?"

"He will", said Fionn, "and be all the better off for it".

They pulled up outside the travel agents and went in together tickets in hand. They were greeted by a bright display of daffodils in the baskets that had previously held Valentines Day sweets. Yellow candles flickered pleasantly in the grate and the whole shop smelt of spring. The office was empty a reflection of the economic situation. Fionn and Liam did not hold out much hope of getting Matthew's money back.

"Morning", said Liam, "we're here with some tickets you sold to a friend of mine for a cruise".

There were three girls behind the desk.

"Matthew, Matthew Ryan's tickets?" Amanda asked.

They all walked over towards Liam and Fionn.

"Sure the poor creator", said Justine coming out of the back office, "how's he holding up?"

"We heard a few hours ago", said Melanie.

"We were hoping that he'd gone ahead on the holiday himself", said Jane. "She seems like a proper bitch". "And we were just saying he was the most romantic man we had ever come across, there aren't many out there that would think of such a Valentine's Day gift".

"Well in fairness it was his first year's anniversary", said Liam.

"Still and all said Justine anniversary or not there isn't many would think or bother to give such an extravagant gift".

"Well, said Liam, we know we may be on a fool's errand but we were wondering if he could get his money back."

"Well", said Justine, "I'm sure ye appreciate I cannot afford to hand over that much money". "The cruise company has already taken the money and under the circumstances if he had cancelled even at a late date there might have been some chance they would have returned the money but as it is they will not give me back the money and I cannot afford to.. . Leave it with me a minute let me think I'd like to help him my heart goes out to him but there's no way I can afford to be handing out six thousand from my own pocket". "To be honest I haven't got it".

"The fool", said Fionn, "he didn't spend that much did he?"

"Oh yeah", said Justine, "two weeks total luxury doesn't come cheep". "I can't see the cruise company compensating him in any way, of course I'll contact them but I know they won't".

They all fell silent and Justine racked her brains thinking what can I do. Ormond radio was playing away in the background. “So why don’t you ring in and tell us you Valentine’s day stories maybe he forgot to get you flowers, maybe he burned down the kitchen, you could have got engaged ring in and let us know how the day went for you, said the girl talking to Theo Bishop on Ormond radio” .

“And when is it again your show starts, asked Theo?”

“Saturday”, replied Patricia, “the same time slot as your own”. “Leanne is manning the phone right now, we are expecting a lot of calls so unfortunately we won’t be able to put everyone on the air, so ring in and tell us your stories”.

“Indeed do, said Theo, and you could be live on the air with the lovely Patricia”.

“Thanks for coming in and talking to us Patricia and we’ll be right back after this piece of music from the beautiful Beyonce “If I were a boy”.

“That’s it, said Justine, if he’ll help me get a bit of publicity that will boost my sales I’ll give him a credit note for the full amount”. “We both come out winners, Matthew gets to book another holiday going away right now might be just the thing he needs and my shop may get some much needed custom”. “

Publicity how do you mean”, asked Liam?

“Well”, said Justine, “say he rings in Ormond radio in the morning and he tells his story and they put him on the show Saturday of course he would have to include how he got a credit note from us for the full amount”.

“Oh, said Fionn, I don’t know about that we will have to ask Matthew and what makes you think Ormond radio would be interested?”

“Oh they would be were you not listening? What Valentine’s Day story could top that?”

“Well”, said Liam, “we will ask him and let you know”.

Liam and Fionn turned tickets in hand and headed back to Matthew’s house only to find him surrounded by women making him tea wrapping blankets around him urging him to take a half one for the shock of it all, asking if he would like to go to bed they could turn on the blanket for him. Matthew seemed more alert and less in shock. He told his story over and over again to the women that surrounded him always emphasizing how happy they were, how much he loved her. How they should have gone on a lovely Valentines Day meal and how they should now be on board a luxury liner on their way to cruise the Caribbean for two weeks. The girls who surrounded him ohed and awed in all the right places and Liam wondered when he had last seen so many single women in the one room. Mrs. O'Brien looked at Fionn and Liam and winked delighted.

"That will give him a boost, she said, shows him that there are more fish in the sea". With a smile of satisfaction Mrs. O'Brien turned to leave, "I've got to go put on the dinners for the kids I'll talk to ye later but tell me this before I go did ye get the poor fool any of his money back".

Matthew heard her and blushed at being called a fool.

"That's something we have to talk to Matthew about", said Fionn.

"Yeah", said Liam, it's all up in the air at the minute.

"Go on", said Matthew, "what is it?"

"Well", said Liam, "the cruise company won't give you anything but Justine will give you a credit note for the full amount if you'll go on Ormond radio and tell your story and say how good Justine was to give you the credit note".

"But", said Fionn remember it's your own choice.

"I'll do it", said Matthew, "I'll burn her, I'll burn the bitch everyone will know what she did".

"Are you sure", said Liam," if you do this it will make reconciliation next to impossible?"

"Reconciliation", scoffed Matthew, "I don't want any reconciliation with that bitch". The girls were silent and turned to leave.

"Hold on a minute Yvonne I want a word with you". "Why are you not in school? And also did you know about this and not tell me the other day when I was in getting my hair done??"

"No, no said Yvonne I just know how she talks about you". "I was in Catriona's office over the fashion show one day when you sent Claire flowers and sweets at work".

"Why are you here?"

"I came up with my friends".

"Those women are way too old for you to be hanging around with". "Does your mother know where you are?"

" I can go where I like I just came up here to say I was sorry for what happened to you, and for your information Tom is my godfather, but I'm sorry I came now I'm off".

"Ah no", said Mathew, "I didn't mean to jump down your throat think that's the second time I've done that". "It seems you were right about her after all maybe I should be taking advice from you".

"Yvonne laughed", "its ok I seem to get the same reaction from a lot of people, and I've got to go anyway".

"Ok so Yvonne", said Matthew, "sure I'll see you again especially if I'm going to do this show thing for your mammy".

"Bye so", said Yvonne, "talk to you".

"If you're sure so said Liam we'll get on to Justine and let her know and get on with organizing this thing".

"I'll ring her myself", said Matthew, have you got the number handy.

Fionn pulled out his mobile and called out the number to Matthew who typed it into his phone and dialed.

"Hi is that you Justine it's me Matthew Ryan".

" Hi Matthew", said Justine, "I'm so sorry for what's happened to you, its terrible how are you holding up of course you must be in terrible shock still, what a bombshell". "Yeah it was, it was the last thing I would have expected". "We were so happy, and once again Matthew was squealing like a pig".

"Oh I'm so sorry Matthew", said Justine, "why don't you take a while for yourself think about it, your friends must be barely in the door". "Think about it for a day or two and then get back to me she hung up".

Justine felt a lump in her throat and began to feel guilty what kind of person was she, she was willing to exploit this man's pain for advertising, but then again she thought these are recessionary times and I'm going to hand over a credit note for six thousand euro. Sweet Jesus fuck me pink what am I thinking I'd need to get a lot of people in the door to make this worth while. I hope he doesn't do it I'm ruined. What am I going to do? Relax, Justine told herself he won't spend it all in the one go. Hopefully it will last him a few years, I'll make it valid for five years. I'll take him out to lunch and make sure he knows to mention my business as often as possible. Sweet Jesus I'm ruined. The phone rang again.

"Hello", said Justine.

"Hello its Matthew again listen Justine I'm going to do this I think it's a great idea even if I never got a credit note".

"Shit thought Justine I shouldn't have offered the credit note so". "I'm going to go over there and tell the world or at least the county what some women are like, what she's like". "I'll burn her I tell you, and that two faced Dave lets see what the world thinks of him when I'm through with my story".

"It's only Ormond radio Matthew", said Justine, "the world won't hear it". "Be sure you're not doing something you'll regret later". "Tell you what I'll go speak with the Ormond radio team, there is a girl Leanne they are saying to call and tell your story to I'll see what she has to say and get back to you".

Justine hung up the phone and rang directory enquires and got the number for Ormond radio. She dialed the main reception a man answered the phone.

"Hello my name is Justine and I was ringing as I heard the lady Patricia on the radio this morning she was looking for people to ring in and tell how their Valentine's Day went".

"No problem", he replied, "I have the number right here 087/123456. "Best of luck with it now Justine hope you get on the air". "Thanks", said Justine, "but it's not me it's for a customer".

But the man who answered the phone was already gone. Justine dialed the number it was engaged, she dialed again engaged. It took her three hours before she got through. Finally the phone rang it was answered on the first ring.

"Hello Leanne here can I take your details".

"Hello my name is Justine but it's not my Valentine's Day story I want to tell you. I own a travel agents shop and it's a customers story I'm ringing about he would go on air himself though".

"I don't know, said Leanne, if your customer wants to tell his Valentines Day story why couldn't your customer ring in?"

"Oh Leanne he wanted to but I said I'd ring for him and see if ye were interested it's the saddest and best story ye will have".

"I don't know, said Leanne, there's a lot of good stories coming in".

"But", said Justine, "this man just found out on Valentines Day that his wife was having an affair with his best friend, the best man at his wedding".

"Oh", said Leanne.

"Yeah", said Justine, "and not only was it Valentines Day it was their anniversary".

"The poor guy", said Leanne.

"Oh Leanne", said Justine, "there's more he had just shelled out six thousand euros to me for a luxury cruise of the Caribbean". "It was a big surprise he'd organized the time off work and all for her, without her knowing". "He had a table booked for them for a meal for Valentines night". "He planned to give her the tickets over desert but they never got to the restaurant". "He came home early to surprise her but he was the one who got the surprise and not the nice kind". "They were there on the couch at it you get me".

"And", said Leanne, "is he willing to come on air and tell all this?"

"Yes, yes", said Justine, "and as a good will gesture my travel agents are at our own expense giving him a credit note for six thousand euros". "Money that he spent on a cruise he never got to go on". "Also we are willing to give a fifty euro voucher to the first twenty people through the door to book a holiday but it must be on the day of the show, and they must spend over two hundred euros".

"Well", said Leanne, "it sounds a little heavy I don't know what kind of show Patricia wants to put on maybe she's leaning more towards the humorous side". "I think it's a great story and freebies there is no better way to get people to stay tuned". "If it was up to me however I'd say we have a cracking show". "I'll get on to Patricia and her production team and I'll be back to you, can I take your number?"

Justine gave Leanne her number not twenty minutes later her phone rang.

"Hi", is this Justine?

"Yes it is who is this?"

"This is Patricia from Ormond radio I believe you were just on to Leanne".

"Yeah", said Justine, I was so I take it this is good news to hear from you so quickly?"

"Yeah", said Patricia I'm thinking of having your customer do this show and make it more about the stress caused by celebrations be it Valentine's Day, Easter, Christmas, Communions or Confirmations". "I'm going to have someone a councilor or someone on the show as well giving advice; hopefully I'll be able to find someone". "But first I am going to have to hear your customer tell his story in his own words". "Take down this number and get him to ring me tomorrow between ten and five".

Justine took down the number, "right Patricia I have that I'll pass on the number and ask him to contact you".

"Thanks", said Patricia for contacting us, and for the vouchers all that remains now is to make sure he won't bore the listeners to death and have them changing stations".

"Fine", said Justine, "I'll be on to him straight away".

Matthew sat on his bed Fionn, Liam, Kevin and Damien had convinced him to get some rest before they left.

How on earth did they think I could sleep, Matthew thought and my heart broken? Why don't they understand? And forcing me to eat how can I eat and my stomach in knots? He stared at the screen of his mobile at the screen saver of him and Claire. He held the phone to his ear and dialed. Claire's number rang and rang and then went to voice mail, she wouldn't answer the phone to him. He put his number on private and tried again, still no answer. He left message after message for her. Claire baby I love you come back we can work things out. I know its Dave's fault come home I love you we need never mention this again. Finally he lay back on the pillows exhausted he must have rang her fifty times. The least she could do was return his calls, he thought. But exhaustion did not deter him he continued to dial and dial, just as tiredness was about to overtake him and he was about to fall asleep the phone rang. He looked at the number private. Hello, he answered hopefully let it be her let it be her he thought.

"Hello, this is Dave, Matthew you've got to leave Claire and I alone we've moved on you've got to start afresh and stop ringing Claire's number she is finding this all very upsetting". "We are not saying there won't be a time when we can all be in contact again even friends if that is what you want but for now we need you to leave us alone to build a life together we've moved on".

"Put Claire on the phone", said Matthew, "I want to talk to Claire".

"You're not listening", said Dave, "I've told you we've moved on we're starting a new life together one that for the moment does not include you".

"Don't talk shite"; said Matthew, "it's been two days". "You've turned her head with your bullshit stories but you mark my words she will see right through you sooner rather than later and she'll be back home to me". "And I'll be waiting for her with open arms because I know this is your fault".

"Jesus Matthew", said Dave, "cop yourself on for fucks sake now you listen here to me if you keep ringing her number Matthew we will just have to change the number", and the phone went dead Dave hung up.

Matthew knew what he would do he would go on Ormond radio and declare his undying love for Claire. She would hear how much he loved her and come back. She was in some kind of crisis and he'd missed it, this wasn't what she wanted it was a cry for help. He'd just have to hang in there and all would work it's self out. They would tell their grandchildren this story in years to come and laugh and say what a slimy bastard that Dave was and how neither of them knew where he was now. Matthew fell asleep whishing all kinds of disaster on Dave. This was his fault entirely, well thought Matthew let's see how he manages without access to my wallet pathetic fool he's going to end up alone and friendless bastard. It was dawn when Matthew woke up must be nearly eight in the evening he thought, he turned and looked at the clock on the bedside table it was six in the morning. Holy shit thought Matthew I've slept for fifteen hours, hows that happened to me. He picked up his mobile phone five missed calls from a number he didn't know. Claire he thought quickly dialing his voicemail, he listened deflated.

"Hello", this is Justine I was in contact with Ormond radio and I have a number for you to ring tomorrow between ten am and five". "They would be very interested in you telling your story but they want to hear it in your own words".

Matthew began to cheer up that was great he would be able to talk to Claire through the radio he was sure it was Dave's fault she didn't answer the phone to him. He lay in bed imagining the interview in his head.

Patricia would say to him so Matthew I see from my notes here that you are still very much in love with this woman. Claire, Patricia, he would say. Her name is Claire. Oh sorry Matthew, Patricia would reply, Claire I see you are still very much in love with Claire. Yes I am Patricia; we are perfect together did you ever see that film vanilla sky that's what it's like for me she completes me. Awe, Matthew, Patricia would reply that's so sweet I see you are definitely a new man so sensitive and in touch with your feminine side. I try Patricia I try, Matthew would reply and Patricia would then hold up her hand to stop him as he went on to talk. Sorry to interrupt you there Matthew, she would say but we have someone on the line very anxious to talk to you. Patricia would then flick a switch and Claire would be live on air talking to him. Oh Matthew, Claire would say how could I have done this to you can you forgive me and take me back? Of course honey Matthew would reply and all the Ormond radio staff would be on their feet shouting and clapping and congratulating them saying things like sure ye were obviously the perfect couple ye were bound to get back together.

Matthew felt as though only a few minutes had passed since he had woken up when his daydreaming was interrupted by knocking at the front door. He ran down the stairs and opened the door it must be Claire at this hour she must not like to let herself in after what's happened, as if I'd mind. He opened the door and his face fell with disappointment it was Mrs. O'Brien with a fry for him for his breakfast.

"Oh she said noting the disappointment on his face I'm not who you expected am I?" "Good morning Mrs. O'Brien you're too good making me breakfast like this and all the help you've given me over the past few days why would I be anything other than happy to see you?"

"Ah sure your more than welcome", said Mrs. O'Brien.

But inside Matthew was thinking you interfering cow if you hadn't run Claire from here yesterday she'd be back with me already. Will you come in Mrs. O'Brien asked Matthew.

"Ah not now Matthew I've to organize the children but if your lonely out here at any stage come out to me my lot won't be long occupying you". "Just drop the plate back when you're finished there's no rush and again if you want anything you know where I am".

Matthew carried the plate into the kitchen stepped on the pedal bin and dumped the contents of the plate in the bin. He couldn't face food right now.

5

Claire sat at the kitchen table eating breakfast in Dave's apartment.

"I can't believe how they treated you there yesterday", said Dave, "refusing to give you back your clothes that's just childish".

"Don't worry", said Claire, "I won't be long softening his cough let him keep all my clothes he may go all tranny and wear them around the house for all I care". "I've got the credit cards and bank card". "I'll clean him out so I will". "I'm heading to the bank link machine and I'm going to take every penny he has got".

"I don't know", said Dave, "what we did to him and to take his money as well it doesn't sit easy with me". "If it was anybody else, but not Matthew".

"Give it more time it's only the third day since all this blew up give him until next week and I'm sure he'll give you back your clothes jewelry or whatever it is you want".

"It's not him", said Claire, "I could walk all over that fool it's that auld biddy next door, took at me with the brush so she did I was afraid she'd fall on me and I'd wake up in Australia". "No, no Dave I've made up my mind besides it's not all his money some of it's mine in fact half after all I am his wife". "I'm entitled to half of everything".

"How much do you think there is in there, Dave asked?"

"I'm not sure", said Claire, "maybe twenty or thirty thousand and we just paid the credit card bills so another twenty maybe between the two of them".

"God", said Dave that would really set us up and you'll only take half?"

"Yeah, yeah, said Claire, I'll teach him to leave me walking around in men's clothes". Still in men's clothes this time a rugby shirt and sweat pants Claire headed for the bank link machine.

I'll take every cent he has she thought, it would be easier to go into the bank to take the money from the account but I'll empty the credit cards first from the machine in Tesco's.

Claire walked in the door of the supermarket there was no one at the machine she walked over stuck in the first credit card and typed in the number. She choose display balance from the menu. Your balance is 10,000 euro the amount you may withdraw today is 10,000 euro. Do you require any further services: the screen asked her yes or no? Claire pressed yes. On the screen different options jumped up from 20 to 200 euros, below this on the screen it said other amounts. Claire selected this option, she then typed in ten thousand euros'. The maximum you may withdraw from this machine is E500. Do you still wish to proceed? Claire pressed yes, and out came her first 500 euros'. She repeated this ten times before a notice came up on the machine, we regret this machine is out of order. With 5,000 euros' in her pocket Claire left Tesco and headed for Dunne's stores where she repeated the process leaving with another 5,000 euros' and another empty bank link machine. She then went to the service station beside Dunne's and inserted the other credit card. Your balance is 4,000 euro do you wish to proceed. Claire pressed yes, what the fuck did he spend 6,000 euros on she thought to herself. Again different amounts were displayed on the machine below these were other amounts. Claire clicked on other amounts and typed in 4,000 euros', the maximum you may withdraw from this machine is E400 do you still wish to proceed? Claire pressed yes and repeated this process until the machine was empty and saying we regret this machine is out of service. She left with another 3,600 euros in her pocket. Now with thirteen thousand six hundred euros in her purse Claire was finding it difficult to close the zip. Ah here thought Claire he can keep the 400 euros it's too much bother to take it out, I'll go empty the bank account. Claire went into the bank of Ireland she decided to check the balance first she put the card into the mini statement machine entered the pin and waited.

The small piece of paper flew out at her she caught it in her hand and stared in disbelief balance 250,000 euros. That's not possible she thought and put the card in and requested another statement. Balance 250,000 euros she read again oh my God we're rich. She walked over and took a withdrawal slip from the counter filled it out for 200,000 euros and went to the desk, she didn't want to empty the account completely incase it aroused suspicion. Without question the lady stamped her withdrawal slip and sent her upstairs to the cashiers who dealt with amounts greater than a thousand euros. She smiled in delight, how could she ever have guessed when she said to Matthew that they should use his account and she would close her original account that it was the best thing she could ever have done. I've only taken 200,000 euros she said to herself ten minutes later as she left the bank her bag heavy with money. I haven't cleaned him out completely that's what the fool gets for not canceling the cards he knew I had them he handed them to me.

Matthew looked at the clock on the kitchen wall ten past ten he picked up the land line and called the number Justine had left for him the previous evening. It was answered on the second ring.

"Hello", Patricia speaking.

"Hi Patricia it's me Matthew you were talking to Justine about me telling my story on your show Saturday".

"Matthew", said Patricia "thanks so much for getting back to me so quickly". "If you're willing we have discussed a show format here at this end and we are thinking of making your story the main body of our show". "But first how are you feeling? Can you tell me what happened in your own words I know Justine told me your story yesterday but I'd just like to hear it from you, from the horses' mouth so to speak".

"I'd be glad to", said Matthew, "see I know she loves me and she will come back to me I just know it". "And Matthew told his story he'd been telling it for a few days now even so he was reduced to tears as he neared the end.

Great thought Patricia this will real them in, and hopefully he will cry again when we broadcast.

"Right so Matthew which would you be most comfortable with would you like to come into the studio or would you prefer to ring in?" "The way we are planning to do the show at the minute is a live interview with you and if you're up to it we would take calls from the public you know people who might want to ask you questions". "So Matthew what do you say?"

"I'll come into the studio and I'd be more than glad to take live calls".

Oh thought Matthew it's just how I imagined it.

"We think your story will touch people", said Patricia, "we're very excited about it here it has the makings of a great first show". "I'll get back to you and let you know what time to be here at give you directions and all". "I'll phone you tomorrow morning". "Is that ok with you Matthew?"

"Yeah", he replied, "its perfect talk to you then".

"Ok bye for now", said Patricia, and hung up.

Matthew was excited about it now too. He was sure that it would be all he needed to get Claire back. All he had to do was wait for Saturday and today was Tuesday. He knew what he would do; he would go into town and get himself new clothes. I wonder should I get my hair done again maybe Emmet could style it. He would go to the chemist and buy Claire that perfume she loved for a welcome home present. He went to the kitchen drawer where he kept an envelope with emergency money in it, he counted it 980 euros I'll really have to sort out something with Claire about the bank account. Ah he thought she will probably be back by Sunday anyway. He looked around the neighbors had the house shining they were great, how could he of thought of Mrs. O'Brien like that she had only been upset for him that was sweet. I'm very lucky and this is only a hiccup every relationship goes through it. Matthew decided he wouldn't bother going back to work until the following week. That would be time enough he would spend until Saturday sprucing himself up to let Claire see what she almost gave up. She must be missing me terribly by now thought Matthew, oh well let her suffer a bit after what she's done to me. Matthew went into town and walked around all the men's clothes shops and ended up coming home with four big bags of clothes. Now he understood why women had so many clothes, he felt great after all the shopping reinvigorated and happy. He went home sat down and watched television and despite all that had happened he felt great secure in the knowledge that Claire would be home Saturday or maybe before then you never know. Seorsha called in after he finished for the day they ordered themselves a Chinese sat back and watched television and had a few cans. Matthew told Seorsha about the radio show but didn't tell him about how he thought it would bring Claire home to him, he wouldn't understand.

"Is that not a bit like airing your dirty linen in public", said Seorsha, "do you not think that you'll regret it".

"No, no", said Matthew, "I'm not going to say anything bad about her just tell my story and say how much I love her and how I understand that she just made a mistake".

Seorsha fell quiet what could he say to that well a lot but he didn't think Matthew was yet ready for that. Seorsha watched the film and Matthew was lost in a world of his own maybe we should still go on a holiday he thought. Would probably be just what we both need. Claire has made a silly mistake that's all; everything will be back to normal before long. At 1am Seorsha went home to his auntie Sheila's to bed and Matthew went up to bed. Wednesday tomorrow he thought Claire will be home by Sunday three days to go. Wednesday morning at eleven o' clock the phone rang it was Patricia from Ormond radio.

"Good morning Matthew how are you this is Patricia".

"Good morning he replied woken by the phone call". He was amazed by how much he was sleeping these days.

"Oh I'm sorry did I wake you?"

"No, no he lied I was awake already".

"So Matthew this is the plan firstly have you an email account".

"Yeah", said Matthew its Mattie@ aol.com.

"Grand", said Patricia, "I've just forwarded you directions to the station".

"It's ok", said Matthew, "I'm from town I know where you are".

"I know that", said Patricia, "but I've sent you the code to access the car park". "Its tricky to find the back entrance, its down a lane better you have directions". "Now this is the plan can you be in the studio for 9am we go on air at ten". "Would you like us to use another name for you or will you be using your own name?" "We would advise you to use a different name as it will protect your identity also if you are involved in legal proceedings down the line it would probably be better".

"No, no, said Matthew it's very important to me that I use my own name Claire always listens to the radio in the morning I want her to hear me I want her to know how much she means to me".

"Okay", said Patricia, "but will it be ok with you to sign a document stating that we advised you to change your name but you refused".

"I will", said Matthew, "there will be no problem there though we will be back together before the week is out".

"With any luck", said Patricia.

That wouldn't make a bad show either thought Patricia I could have them both in studio to talk about how they saved their relationship, but one step at a time Patricia she thought.

"Now I will be there with you so don't worry I will guide you through the whole thing". "Have you ever been interviewed before?"

"No, said Matthew I've never even been in a radio station".

"Oh right", said Patricia. "We had hoped to have a councilor in the studio as well but it was to last minute and we couldn't get anyone". "But from your side all that remains is for you to turn up on Saturday". "Are you sure you want to do this Matthew it isn't to late for us to change the program layout?"

"No, no", said Matthew, "I would be happy to do it I'm sure".

"Fine so Matthew", said Patricia, "we will take it as a done deal so I'll see you at nine Saturday and don't be nervous it will be fine". "Oh and don't forget to open your email with the directions we don't want to be getting you lost".

Matthew spent Thursday morning cleaning the house and doing his washing. At twelve o'clock he text Mrs. O'Brien, Shelia, Seorsha, Fionn, Kevin, Liam, Billy and Damien. He texted Justine. I'm making a big stew nothing fancy a few bottles of wine can ye make it. He told Justine to bring her staff with her, Melanie, Jane and Amanda if she could. Mrs. O'Brien was the first to contact back.

"Jesus Matthew there is a good few of us are you sure I'd have to bring the children". "Of course said Matthew I wouldn't have it any other way. I have chicken nuggets and chips for them. And I have romantica ice cream for us and sweets and smartie ice cream for them. I'll mash some potatoes and stew together for little Hanna would that be ok for her?"

" Jesus Matthew that would be great if you're sure what time?"

"What time are they out of school? 3.15 Matthew. Oh I'd say they come home starved what time do you usually eat".

"That doesn't matter Matthew whatever time suits you".

"How's four?"

"Perfect we will see you then".

"Great", said Matthew.

He then texted the time to everyone else to see if it suited. Justine texted back that Yvonne was with her also and that five people was too much to be bringing in on top of him and she didn't feel that would be fair. Matthew rang travels.

"Don't be daft," he said, "the more the merrier".

Matthew called over to Maria and Anna and they said they would be delighted. Damien, Billy, Kevin, and Fionn were delighted they didn't mind knocking off early. Liam said it suited him great as the restaurant opened at five. Seorsha said it was a great idea he'd get a crate of bud. And Shelia was glad to be out of the house. Shelia said she would come down to give a hand Matthew was delighted to have the company.

He rang Mrs. O'Brien "have you to go down to the school to collect the boys?

"Yeah", she said.

"Well Shelia is here with me why don't I drive you down to collect them?"

"Ah thanks Matthew but I like to get the fresh air and it's dry today but you know what you could do for me, you could mind Hanna whilst I go down if that would be ok".

"It would be great I'll but on the kettle come in for a cup of coffee Shelia and me have everything sorted there is going to be a good few of us it will be great".

Shelia and Matthew brought down extra chairs from Shelia's house and he brought in the small table from the kitchen to the dining room. Mrs. O'Brien called in and had a cup of coffee before she went for the boys.

"This was a great idea Matthew", said Shelia.

"Ah", said Matthew, "I want to say thank you to every one". "You've all been great" "I've got three boxes of red wine in the press in the kitchen I think that will be enough."

"More than enough", said Mrs. O'Brien. "I'm off for the kids".

"Come straight here", said Matthew.

"I'll just get them to change their clothes", said Mrs. O'Brien, "they have school tomorrow, I'm hoping to get another day out of the uniforms".

Maria and Anna arrived in the door as Perpetual was leaving.

"We said we would come over early to help what can we do", asked Anna?

" Nothing", said Matthew, "the stew is cooked on the range and the table is set".

"Come on and the four of us will open a bottle of wine."

At half three Damien, Kevin, Billy and Fionn arrived. Next Mrs. O'Brien came They had bottles of wine open and Shelia filled glasses while Matthew sat at the table feeding baby Hanna stew and potatoes. Don't worry Perpetual I put no salt in it. Your grand Matthew, said Mrs. O'Brien its great to have all this done for you. Have a glass of wine Perpetual said Shelia ah I'll not said Mrs. O'Brien I have the little ones. Jesus said Fionn isn't there enough of us here we will see that the boys are ok relax for a while cant you its not as if your going to get drunk. Matthew sat Hanna on the duvet he had brought from the spare bedroom and handed her, her toys from the pram he also gave her a saucepan and wooden spoon.

"That's great music", said Kevin.

"What's all this", said Seorsha, "walking into the kitchen?"

The oven beeped.

"That's the chicken nuggets and chips boys I've got a table set up for ye here sit down and I'll get the dinner out for ye". "7up or orange juice boys?"

"7up".

"Would you like tomatoes sauce for those chips?"

"Yes please", they replied.

Just then there was a knock at the door and Liam came in. "Am I late he asked?"

"Not at all", said Shelia, as she put a glass of wine in his hand.

Just as he had given up hope on them Justine and Yvonne, Melanie, Jane and Amanda arrived in the door.

"Where is your partner?" Matthew asked, "he was welcome to come too did I forget to say".

"Ah", said Justine, "he is ok he is happy at home in front of the television".

Matthew then took the stew potatoes and vegetables from the main oven where they had been keeping warm, and placed them on the table Shelia had set earlier. By half four they were all seated at the table eating laughing and drinking. It was so much fun that Liam didn't bother going in to the restaurant but rang the head waitress and asked her to lock up for him. At eight o'clock Mrs. O'Brien went home with the children. Matthew walked her to the door.

"Thanks for your company for the evening", said Matthew, "we need to do this more often".

"That would be lovely," said Mrs. O'Brien, "it would be lovely".

"Here", said Matthew, "give herself here to me I'll carry her in to the house for you and put her to bed".

"Matthew will you read us a story", asked Cian?

"Oh would you", said Ciaran?

"I will", said Matthew, "just a quick one".

"You will not", said Mrs. O'Brien, "go back into your company boys home into your pj's and bed now or no supermacs Saturday".

The two boys ran in home and Matthew laughed he and Mrs. O'Brien walked in behind them and Matthew carried a sleeping Hanna upstairs and put her into the cot.

"Thanks Matthew", said Mrs. O'Brien, "I'll just change her now and put a baby grow on her I'd say she won't wake for the night".

"Goodnight Perpetual", said Matthew, and he headed back out home where a sing song was in progress".

It was four am when everyone went home and Matthew went to bed exhausted yet he was wide awake at seven am.

Friday eight in the morning and Matthew was in the shower , he decided to treat himself to a wet shave he would pay Emmet a visit, if Yvonne was there he could get her too fill her mother in on what was happening with the show. He decided to shave himself altogether and go to Travels and fill Justine in, in person.

"Oh Matthew", said Justine, "when he walked in the door I was going to ring you to ask you to come down to meet up I was going to offer to take you to lunch thanks so much for the other day it was lovely".

Melanie and Amanda looked up from the desks where they were working.

"Yeah Matthew it was great craic thanks".

"Yvonne was very taken with the children she thought the baby was dead cute". "I must give you her number for Mrs. O'Brien if she ever needs a hand wants to go out or anything Yvonne would baby sit for her". "Jesus she is a great woman for her age". "She's a legend", said Matthew, "they don't make them like that anymore". "Lunch sounds good", said Matthew.

"Matthew when your on Ormond radio won't you be sure to mentioned us loads".

"Oh don't worry", said Matthew, "I'll mention you loads and then when Claire hears me and comes home I'll take you out to lunch, the lot of you to thank you anywhere you want".

Matthew could say that here, he was amongst woman they will understand he thought. Justine was struck speechless surely he wasn't for real like nah he couldn't be that stupid.

"Matthew", said Justine, "you know going on this show will probably piss Claire off not have her running back to your arms?"

Matthew laughed.

"No not at all you don't know her besides I'm going to tell my story but I'm going to say how I understand it's a mistake nothing we can't overcome but that Dave he's a different kettle of fish that one".

"Okay said Justine come on we'll go for lunch I know it's early but we can call it brunch".

"Fine by me", said Matthew.

They went to the Tea Rooms the shop was all but empty there were only two other people there. They sat down on one of the red leather seats and Matthew was surprised how easy it was to talk to Justine. He found himself forgetting Claire for the half hour they talked. She spoke of Yvonne, the travel agents but she seemed lost in thought at times kind of preoccupied. I wonder what's bothering her thought Matthew.

Saturday morning Matthew lay out the new clothes he would wear into the studio for the interview on the bed the brown jack and jones t shirt the Calvin Kline jeans and his cream zip up sweater casual but smart. He had a shower and then shaved splashed himself in power for men and put on his new clothes. He was nervous now and his stomach felt sick did he really want to share his story with the whole county.

"Hello, hello he heard from a voice down stairs". "It's only us old ones", shouted up Perpetual.

Matthew could hear Shelia laughing. He could tell from the voices that they were in the doorway.

"Come in sit down I'm delighted ye are here I want a second opinion on my clothes". "Ah would you go on", said Shelia.

"Would you look at that", said Mrs. O'Brien and Shelia whistled as Matthew walked down the stairs.

"Ah Shelia if we were only twenty years younger".

Matthew smiled, "so I look ok so?

"You're looking like a male model", said Shelia.

"Jesus Matthew", said Mrs. O'Brien you scrub up well doesn't he Shelia.

"Yeah", Shelia replied, "and you smell well too is that the new lynx".

"No", said Matthew, "its power for men" by 50 cent.

"Well, said Shelia, you look great and you smell great it's a pity it's not television".

"Ah", said Mrs. O'Brien, "you'll come home from the station with a new woman maybe". "You never know", said Matthew, "I might bring the old one back with me". The women looked at each other exchanged a look and fell silent.

"So, said Matthew, can I get you ladies a cup of coffee or some breakfast?"

" That's why we are here", said Mrs. O'Brien, Shelia has a big fry all ready in hers' the kids are down there with Seorsha wanting to whish you luck on your radio debut".

"God", said Matthew, "that's so good of you Shelia".

"She's the best", said Mrs. O'Brien; "I don't know what I'd do without her".

"And me", said Matthew, "I don't know what I'd do without the two of ye". "I'll just grab a hoodie to put over my clothes so I don't destroy them the morning that's in it I'm bound to drop egg all down my front."

Matthew ran up the stairs two at a time.

"Honestly ladies ye can't imagine how much this means to me".

Shelia smiled sadly at Mrs. O'Brien

"Sure God help us", she said, and the two women looked down at the carpet. Two seconds later Matthew bounded back down stairs he linked each of the women by the arm and they walked the two doors up and into Shelia's house, the smell of cooked breakfast greeted them before they went inside Matthew's stomach rumbled he was going to enjoy this he couldn't remember the last time he felt hungry. They walked in the door Seorsha was stood over the frying pan cooking the eggs.

"This is too much trouble", said Matthew, "but I can't but say I'm delighted, but really ye must have been up at the crack of dawn".

"Sure", said Mrs. O'Brien, I'm always up at the crack of dawn with the children and Shelia is an early riser and Seorsha worked last night he's not long in".

Seorsha turned around, "how's our newest celebrity?

"Can we get your autograph, asked Cian?

"Yeah ,said Ciaran, "when your famous".

"Can we tell all the kids at school we know you, asked Ciaran?

"Yeah not a bother", said Matthew.

He wasn't nervous anymore Hanna woke up in her pram crying.

"Can I pick her up Perpetual", asked Matthew?

"Go for it", said Mrs. O'Brien.

Matthew held Hanna in his arms and her warmth swept over him.

"You're a great woman Mrs. O'Brien".

"Nah", she replied, what am I doing that is so great aren't I blessed with each one of them". They sat down to the big fry of bacon and eggs sausages beans mushrooms and toast. Cian and Ciaran sang the jumbo breakfast roll.

"8.30", said Matthew, "I hate to break this up but I had better be going".

"Can I go with you?" asked Cian.

"I don't mind", said Matthew, "he will be company for me".

"I would let him go with you with a heart and a half Matthew but he's not dressed or washed or anything", said Mrs. O'Brien.

"That will tell you how distracted I am I never even noticed you were both in your pajamas". I'll tell you what why don't we all go to the cinema this evening and to supermacs as well instead how does that grab everyone my treat? Go on Ladies when's the last time ye were at the cinema? What do you reckon Seorsha an evening of pg rated fun?"

"Fine", said Mrs. O'Brien, but where will I get a babysitter for Hanna?"

" Leave it with me I'll be ringing Justine her daughter Yvonne is fifteen I'll ask her if she'll baby-sit?"

"Oh, said Mrs. O'Brien do you think she'd be ok, she seemed a nice young one the other night but is she used to babies".

"She's a mad young one but yeah I'd say she'll be fine actually I'd say the two of you would get on great I'll let you know straight after the show when I've been talking to her". "And her mam already said she must give me Yvonne's number for you incase you ever needed a baby sitter". "Well I better head before I'm late I've to be there for nine".

Matthew left and closed the door behind him, ran in home pulled off the sweater that he had luckily put on over his clothes. Brushed his teeth and ran out the door into the car and off down town to be interviewed on Ormond radio. The Valentines Day massacre two that would be a good name for the show thought Matthew. He had never been in a studio before it was a lot more comfortable than he had expected there were computer screens scattered around the place and there was one in front of him on which he could read the texts that had come in for the previous show. Derek the producer showed him around.

"You'll see your own texts and questions on that screen once the program starts". "That's if anyone wants to ring in or text", said Matthew.

They both laughed.

"And if my ex rings in, said Matthew put her on the air".

"By all means", said Derek, "are you expecting her to ring in?"

"Yeah", said Matthew, "I'm expecting her to ring in I'd say she is missing me by now". "Ok", said Derek the main thing is to relax try not to be nervous pretend you're at home having a conversation with your friends". "Patricia will be here in a minute she's just checking the music she's cued for the show has come up ok on the computer". "Have you any questions for me before the show Matthew", asked Derek? "Can I get you a cup of coffee or anything?"

"Ah your grand", said Matthew, "I don't want to have to go out to the toilet during the show, actually could you tell me where the toilets are I'll just pop there before we start". Derek pointed the way and Matthew sighed and headed into the bathroom. He splashed water over his face and the back of his neck he could hear his heart beating in his ears. Keep it together he said over and over in his head. A woman was walking down the corridor towards Matthew as he left the bathroom.

"Matthew", she said, as she approached him her hand extended. "I just came down to make sure you hadn't fainted or anything". "You nervous?"

"Yeah", said Matthew.

"Don't be", said Patricia, "we will take good care of you".

Matthew looked as white as a sheet.

"Come on", said Patricia, "we'll get you sitting down and get you a glass of water".

She sat Matthew on a chair in the studio they would be working from. She walked out to get Matthew a glass of water.

"Jesus Derek he is as white as a ghost what are we going to do". "If this falls through that's our show down the toilet, there may never be a second show".

"Relax would you", said Derek, "one person with stage fright is more than enough". "Isn't he gorgeous", said Patricia, "it's a pity this isn't television".

"Well I better take this water into him, how long before we start?

"Fifteen minutes", said Derek.

"I'd say the sooner the better", said Patricia.

"Here you go", said Patricia, "there is some water for you". "How are you feeling now?"

"I'm very nervous", said Matthew.

"Well don't be just do what you did on the phone with me treat this the same way just tell your story". "If there is any question to much for you, or you get upset I've music queued you give me the nod and I'll throw it on".

"Right", said Matthew, thinking to himself it's too late to run now. I can do this he told himself. It's what I have to do to get Claire back. It's worth it. I can do this. Derek popped his head around the door five minutes to go. Patricia sat on the chair across from Matthew.

"See those headphones there Matthew pop them on you, see that screen in front of you, you will see all the texts coming in on that screen". "Leanne is answering the phones questions phoned in will come up on the screen to so you can give me a nod if it's a question you don't want to answer". "It's the same with anyone who will be put on air Leanne will be talking with them and will know their question and put it up on the screen and you can decide what live callers we have". "So try to relax Matthew you are completely in control".

A voice came in over an intercom in five four three Matthew looked through the glass window Derek was behind it in front of what looked like a mixing desk he was now counting in silence with his fingers two one.

"Hello and welcome to the first show' Your stories with Patricia Cornwall". "For our first show as it's a week since Valentines Day we have a guest in studio to tell us all about his Valentines Day". "I'm warning you ladies have a hankie out there will be tears".

Matthew felt a lump in his throat as the color drained from his face.

Patricia looked over and saw him, oh no, oh no she thought don't freeze on me please god don't freeze on me.

"Good morning Matthew and welcome to the studio".

"Thanks Patricia", replied Matthew, "thank you for having me".

"I believe Valentine's Day is a rather special day for you".

"Yeah Patricia", said Matthew, "it is or should I say it was".

Patricia heaved a sigh of relief, thank God he talked. Matthew was off like a greyhound from the traps.

"See Patricia it was my, our first years anniversary".

"Go on Matthew", urged Patricia, tell us how you planned to spend your valentines day. "I'm telling you ladies you'll be turning green with envy when you hear this one". "Well, said Matthew", as it was our anniversary, and as we were thinking of starting a family the following year, I wanted to do something special to mark not only our anniversary and Valentines Day but also our last year as just us, you know the last year before children". "So I went into travels and met with Justine the owner of the business there". "I'm telling you Patricia if you want to enjoy the experience of booking your holiday Justine in travels is the place to go". "The décor inside and out is fabulous and the service is next to none". "If you were to give a star rating to a travel agents Justine's would be five stars". Justine and Yvonne and Emmet were in the barbers listening to the interview when Matthew was finished his speal about travels they screamed and jumped up and down.

"Well if that's not a ringing endorsement I don't know what is", said Emmet.

"Anyways Matthew continued I booked a two week cruise of the Caribbean". "My wife Claire didn't have a clue". "I booked us a table for dinner and the tickets were to be brought out with the final course".

Claire was on her own in the apartment preparing dinner. She could feel her face burning.

"The bastard he can't do this, there has to be some law against this I'll sue Ormond radio". "I always wanted to go on a cruise feck it".

Claire laughed "I think I can afford a cruise if I want one now". "I'm delighted I took that money now the cheek how dare he go on the radio telling our private business". "Fuck him",

Claire turned off the radio and stared at it for a second then turned it back on and sat in front of it listening. Matthew continued.

"I went to Claire's boss Catriona and she arranged the two weeks off". "Catriona she was a lady she couldn't have been nicer". "Then on Valentines Day I went home to get ready for us to go out, I was home early Patricia and that is where things got messy". "Claire and my so called best friend and best man from our wedding was having I guess I better be careful how I word this Patricia, lets say a bit of how's your father on our couch". "Now they have gone and moved in together". "But Claire I know your out there listening at least I hope you are and I want you to know it's all ok just come home don't go making a mountain out of a mole hill". "I love you it's all going to be ok I promise". "I love you".

The computer screen in front of Matthew began to fill as texts came through and Leanne relayed proposed live questions.

"That was some blow Matthew and only a week ago you must still be in shock, said Patricia, you see in the interest of fairness I wanted to get Matthew on the show ladies and gentlemen to show that it can happen to boys to". "You must feel very betrayed and angry Matthew you must be hating them both right now".

"No not at all Patricia Dave yeah your right I hate him, but no not Claire". "I'm hollow without you babe I feel so empty you are my world please come home".

"Matthew do you want to answer this text here", how are you doing? What are you thinking? From Stephanie.

"Well", said Matthew, "I feel incomplete as if a part of me is missing I'm in a daze". "I don't know what I'd do without my neighbors and friends, can I say a big hello to them all especially Cian, Ciaran and of course little Hanna".

"You've just done it", said Patricia. "It still doesn't feel real to me all this, said Matthew, my whole world has turned upside down in a matter of minutes and it will never be the same again, not unless Claire comes home".

Patricia eyed the computer screen delighted it was filled with comments people were listening.

"Matthew", said Patricia, we've got someone on the line who wants to ask you a question".

Matthew's face lit up Claire?

"No Matthew", said Patricia, "its Mary from the midlands".

"Hello Mary you have a question for Matthew".

"Yeah, said Mary, would you take her back?"

" In a heart beat", Matthew replied, "in a heart beat". "I'm sure we will end up together again eventually there is no doubt in my mind but that she will be back".

" How could you ever trust her again?" Mary asked.

"Mary that's a very good question, said Mathew, and I'm sure Claire is sitting somewhere wondering will he ever trust me again if I go home". "Will he be forever throwing this in my face?" "But Mary of course I'd trust her this is totally out of character and Claire if your listening I would never again mention what happened if you would only come back to me". "Just please come home, I know you didn't mean any harm I know it was Dave's fault". "Claire its ok just come home".

Like a bolt of lightening the screen lit up with new comments.

"Patricia", can I respond to some of those texts.

"Of course you can", said Patricia.

"Anna first did I not notice something was going on". "Well at the time no but now in hindsight yeah there was three Saturdays ago she said she was going in to work but her office is never open of a Saturday". "There was the night she said she would collect me from the pub and never showed". "There was all the times she didn't even want me to sit next to her but I put all these things down to ordinary everyday things like I believed the explanations she gave me I had no reason not to". "Louise you say I have a sexy voice thanks". "Shawna thanks for the offer of a date but like I said earlier I'll eventually be getting back with my wife".

"Matthew I'm afraid we are out of time sorry folks we didn't get to respond to a third of your texts and we didn't get to take hardly any of your phone calls the time just flies". "Maybe we should have Matthew back another time to answer all your questions see how things are doing".

Matthew sat in a daze staring into the distance she never called, she never called he was thinking over and over again in his head. I didn't get to say half the things I wanted to, to her. I should have told her I love her did I say that?

"Matthew, thank you so much for coming into Ormond radio today to share your story". Patricia took off her headphones, Matthew followed her lead.

"Would you like to come to lunch with us Matthew" she asked.

"Ah no thanks all the same", said Matthew, "I want to get home as soon as I can we are all going to the cinema taking the children and going to supermacs".

"Okay so", said Patricia, "maybe some other time".

Matthew stood up to leave.

"Would you come back let's say in a month and let us know how you're doing?"

"Yeah no bother", said Matthew, "I'll text you let you know how I'm getting on I'll probably be back with my wife".

“No Matthew what I’m asking you is to come back on the show and tell us how you’re doing?”

Matthew blushed oh right he said. Matthew had thought that Patricia was just asking him to let her know how he was.

“Yeah sure Patricia I’ll do your show again just text me on the date”.

“Thanks Matthew”, said Patricia, the listeners loved you they really did.

6

Claire sat in Dave's apartment staring at the radio. The prick, the evil bastard I'm so glad I took his money now. When the show was finished Claire picked up the radio and threw it against the wall it broke in two before crashing to the ground. Matthew rang Justine when he got to his car.

"Matthew she answered thank you so much you were great".

"Thanks Justine I have a favor to ask you actually".

"Anything just name it", said Justine.

"Could Yvonne baby-sit for Mrs. O'Brien to night well this evening actually we are gong to take the boys to the cinema?"

"One sec Matthew Yvonne's here I'll put her on to you".

"Hello Matthew".

"Hello Yvonne how do you fancy a bit of babysitting tonight? I'll give you fifty euros". "Yeah", said Yvonne, "who would I be minding?"

"The baby you were playing with in my house the other night".

"Oh that's great, said Yvonne, what time do you want me up at?"

"For five Yvonne we are going to the cinema for the six o clock show. We're seeing Bolt".

"Fine Matthew I'll be there".

"Thanks Yvonne", said Matthew, "bye".

"Bye", said Yvonne, and hung up".

Matthew, Seorsha, Shelia and Mrs. O'Brien and the children went to the cinema and saw Bolt. Afterwards they went to supermacs and then home. Mrs. O'Brien went in home Matthew had insisted on giving Mrs. O'Brien the fifty euros for Yvonne. Yvonne was fast asleep on the sofa. Mrs. O'Brien went out to Matthew.

"Matthew young Yvonne is asleep on the sofa will you ring her mam and ask if it's ok for her to stay the night?"

"Matthew rang Justine and told her that Yvonne was asleep on the sofa in Mrs. O'Brien's was it ok if she stayed the night there".

"That's fine", said Justine; thanks for letting me know whcre she is".

Perpetual went in and made up the bed in the down stairs bedroom, she gently shook Yvonne awake.

" Do you want to stay here tonight Yvonne", I've the bed ready for you in the spare room?

"That would be great I'll just ring my mam".

"Matthew already did she said it's grand".

Half asleep Yvonne went into the bed room and crawled into bed and slept. It was only ten o' clock but Matthew went straight to bed and slept like a log. The clank of the post through the letterbox woke Matthew Monday morning at nine am. Matthew went downstairs and collected the letters. He went into the kitchen and turned on the kettle. He sat at the table and opened the envelopes. The first two were from the bank. Dear Mr. Ryan we are happy to inform you that you application for the re-mortgage of your home has been successful. The 250,000 euro has been lodged to your account as per your loan agreement. If you have any queries please do not hesitate to contact us.

Shit thought Matthew I must contact them and give them back that money it went completely out of my head.

Matthew went upstairs showered put on a nice shirt and trousers and headed to the bank. He went up to the customer's services desk. There were three in the queue in front of him, he thought he would never get to the counter they were so slow. Finally the lady said next please.

"Hi", Matthew said I got a loan paid into my account there and I no longer need it, well a re-mortgage really and I was wondering could it be taken back of course I realize I'll have to pay the interest for the days it was in my account".

"Ok", said the girl behind the desk, do you have your account number and photographic identification with you?"

"Yes", said Matthew, here's my drivers license and the account number is on that receipt there".

"Thanks", said the girl.

The lady typed Matthews's details into the computer.

"And how much was that loan re-mortgaged for sir, the lady asked".

"250,000 euros Matthew replied".

The lady picked up the phone and rang someone.

"Oliver are you free can you come down here and speak with a customer, yes it's important".

That's unusual thought Matthew, but then again maybe not there is probably a lot of paper work to be done to return the money. The lady behind the counter turned to him, Mr. Ryan if you could just take a seat the manager is on his way down to talk with you. Matthew went over to the seating area and waited. Ten minutes later he noticed Oliver at the customer's service desk talking to the girl behind the counter then he turned around and was heading for him hand extended. Matthew knew Oliver he had looked after his account for the last two years it had been Oliver who had set up the re-mortgage for him.

"Come with me Matthew", said Oliver, "and we will take a look at your account". Together they walked into the office and both sat down.

"Matthew I just want to bring your account up here on the screen for you, just to turn it around there a little bit there we go can you see that?"

"Yes" ,Matthew replied.

"You haven't misplaced your bank cards or anything have you?"

Matthew eyed the screen his stomach turned his arms and legs felt heavy, he felt dizzy. He pushed his chair back from the desk and put his head on his knees he thought he was going to faint. Oliver didn't have to say a thing he knew what was coming next. "Matthew, Matthew are you ok?", Oliver asked.

"I've seen it on the screen", said Matthew, "my accounts been cleaned out".

Oliver knew what had happened between Matthew and Claire but surely she hadn't done this.

"Matthew", said Oliver, "have you mislaid your card or could your card have been swiped? "Matthew give me a minute and I'll check the activity on your account".

At this Matthew straightened up maybe it wasn't Claire maybe someone had stolen the cards. Oliver's words had offered a spark of light in the dark cave that was his brain, but the spark was quenched all too soon.

"Oh Matthew we should have asked for two signatures on the withdrawal slip but it's too late now; Claire withdrew 200,000 from the account Wednesday last". "I'm afraid there's nothing we can do about it".

"Jaysus, Jaysus, Jaysus Matthew repeated over and over". "Oh no I'm destroyed how am I going to pay this back". "I'll lose the house I can't even sell it; even if I could it would never make enough money to pay back the loan". "What am I going to do Oliver? What am I going to do? "When we're finished this job we're working on I don't even know if I'm going to have work". "What am I going to do? I don't know, said Oliver flabbergasted I really don't know this puts your mortgage at 2,500 euros a month".

"You'll be ok for the next few months anyways". "Matthew this is an account in both your names both your wages are going into it and Claire is your wife I'm afraid I can't just close it or cancel the cards". "You've got to get yourself a solicitor get the account frozen". "Matthew you've got two credit cards here with us I'll check them while you're here". "Matthew that one has reached its limit was that you?"

"No", said Matthew.

He sat with his head in his hands.

"So has the other one", said Oliver, "I'm sorry Matthew you've been cleaned out". "I'm putting a note on the account that no monies are to be withdrawn without both parties being present that's the best I can do for you". "I know the credit cards are solely in your name I can cancel them even though it's a bit late". "We can transfer the money from what's left in your account and clear the credit card debt that leaves 30,000 euros". "Matthew I'm sorry for what's happened to you".

Matthew sat rocking back and forth in the chair his head in his hands.

"Matthew, Matthew, said Oliver putting a hand on his shoulder, you've got to pull yourself together you have to get a solicitor, you've got to protect yourself come on". Oliver shook Matthew gently.

"Leave me alone can't you, leave me alone",, Matthew roared and then began to sob his heart out.

The door opened and a mans head appeared around it.

"Is everything ok in here?"

"Yeah everything's fine" replied Oliver, "shut the door".

Oliver put his arm around Matthew's shoulder.

"How could they do this to me Oliver, how could they do it?"

"I don't know Matthew mate I don't know I've never come across the like of this before".

Oliver picked up the phone and dialed extension 25.

"Katie can you bring me in two cups of coffee and some nice chocolate biscuits?"

"They were the two most important people in my life". How could they do this Oliver? 'Matthew', replied Oliver. "I don't know how they could have done this but the thing is that it is done, it cannot be changed, but it must be faced and dealt with, you've got good friends and I hope you count me amongst them". "Matthew I hope you'll consider the advise I'm about to give you". "You need to get a solicitor as soon as possible. You've got to get sorted as soon as possible or you will be cleaned out".

"Where will I go?"

"Surely with the building you have a solicitor who handles your business?"

"Yes, yes Malcolm, replied Matthew, I'll call him as soon as I get home".

"No, Matthew, said Oliver, you'll call him now from here".

"Here's the phone".

Matthew took the phone from Oliver and rang Malcolm's office and got his secretary. "Oh hello Matthew yeah I'll make an appointment for you".

"Can it be kind of soon asked Matthew it's urgent".

" I'm afraid the soonest we can see you is next week".

"Matthew give me the phone", said Oliver, Matthew handed the phone over. "Sarah its Oliver Conway here from the bank is Malcolm in his office? I'm afraid he is with a client". "Oh ok thanks for that Sarah you are a great help goodbye".

Oliver rolled his eyes at Matthew and hung up. There was a knock at the door and Katie came in with two cups of coffee when she left Oliver opened his desk and took out a bottle of whiskey.

"I keep it for special occasions, he said, and although this may not be an occasion it certainly constitutes special circumstances".

Oliver poured two generous measures of whiskey into the coffee, passed one to Matthew slainte he said bottoms up. Oliver took his mobile phone from his pocket and scrolled down through the contacts list. Ah here it is he said and pressed the call button. "Hello Malcolm", it's me Oliver no; "no I can still make squash Friday. I'll tell you that secretary of yours has you well protected".

"Why", said Malcolm, "would she not put you through?"

"No said you were with a client".

"Ha, ha said Oliver I should give her a rise so is something wrong what's so important it can't wait until Friday night?"

"I'm contacting you for Matthew Ryan he is in a spot of bother and needs urgent advice".

"I know, said Malcolm I heard the whole story he was very unfortunate, but I have to say I for one was glad to hear she was back on the market, she's a bit of alright that one".

"Matthew is here with me now like I was saying his marriage broke up and he is in a mess he needs legal advice sooner rather than later".

Matthew gulped when he heard this, it was like hearing it out loud made it real this was the moment he would remember for the rest of his life the moment he realized it was all over Claire would never be coming back to him. These were not the actions of someone who wanted to get back with you. For God's sake he thought, these are not even the actions of someone who ever loved you. How did I get it so wrong, what did I do how did I ruin everything.

My marriage is over, my marriage is over he repeated over and over again in his head. "Great thanks Malcolm"; said Oliver, "I'll send him straight down to you".

Oliver turned to Matthew just as he downed the last mouthful of his laced coffee.

"Head straight down to Malcolm he will fit you in now before lunch".

"Thank you, thank you so much, said Matthew how can I ever pay you back?"

"Don't worry about it you'd do the same for me were it the other way around".

"Thanks so much, Matthew said again as he walked out the door thinking I never thought this would happen to me". "I never thought any of this possible".

It was with apprehension that Matthew walked into the solicitor's office. He knew once he walked in that door that was it, the end no going back. His marriage was over. He was overwhelmed with a great wrenching pain akin to a death. He was too sad too heartbroken to be angry. My marriage is over I have to do this or I will be cleaned out Matthew told himself over and over again in his head. Sarah sat at a desk behind glass in the solicitor's office she was not well pleased with being bypassed. She ignored Matthew's presence completely even when he rang the bell for assistance she remained at the computer and never moved. Matthew sat back down and from the chair he was sitting in he could see she was playing poker on the computer on facebook none the less.

Bitch he thought. Oh God I hope I didn't say that out loud.

Sarah turned and eyed Matthew from head to toe with a vicious look on her face.

"Shit", said Matthew, "I mean I'm very sorry I didn't mean you". Then in his head Matthew thought, that's it now she'll never tell Malcolm I'm here and I won't be seen. Malcolm heard the talking outside he opened his office door and popped his head out. "Ah it's you Matthew thought it might be come on in and we'll see what we can do for you".

Matthew stood up and followed Malcolm like a lamb to the slaughter.

"So Matthew take a seat tell me what's the problem?"

"I discovered my wife was having an affair, said Matthew. She left me for my best friend".

"Ouch", said Malcolm.

"I had applied to have the house re-mortgaged to invest in some property development". "I meant to go to the bank to cancel it as the development fell through but it slipped out of my mind". "I had signed the cooling off waver so the money went straight into my account". "This morning a letter came to say the money was in my well our account I had Claire's name put on my account". "There is only 50,000 euros remaining".

"Claire?" asked Malcolm.

"Yes" Matthew replied. "The card to the bank account is still in her possession she took them with her when she left".

"Right, said Malcolm, this is a tricky one. "Whilst what she has done is morally wrong legally it was her account too legally she has done nothing wrong". "I'm afraid the best I can do for you is we can start separation proceedings all assets will be frozen until an amicable agreement is reached". "That means Matthew you will not be able to sell any property". "Your account will be frozen do you understand the implications?" "It's a lot to take in Matthew but it's the only way I can stop Claire from taking the last of the money".

"I do", said Matthew, I do.

"Right said Malcolm go down to the bank and withdraw whatever money you think you'll need to get you by and then come back up here to me".

"I'll have the paper work sorted and ready for you to sign".

"Do you know Claire's address?"

"Yeah", said Matthew, "she's living with Dave I gave him the deposit for the apartment". "What about your lunch?"

"You're grand Matthew I brought something in with me anyway I didn't intend on heading out".

Matthew went back to the bank. He filled out a withdrawal slip for twenty thousand and went to the counter. The lady typed in Matthew's account number.

"Oh she said I'm afraid I can't let you withdraw any money without your wife being present it says here both parties must be present".

"It's ok said Matthew its me who put that request on the account my wife took 200,000 out of that account I didn't want her taking the rest".

"I'm sorry, said the girl I can't stamp this withdrawal slip unless both parties are present".

Matthew walked away from the counter deflated. He never thought to look for Oliver. Despondency swept over him. He returned to Malcolm's office. Malcolm was behind the glass partition talking to Sarah and came straight out to Matthew.

"So have you that done", asked Malcolm, "just getting Sarah to type up a letter to Claire".

"I couldn't get the money", Matthew replied, "when I was down at the bank before I came here Oliver and me we put a note on the account saying both parties must be present to withdraw money".

"Did you ask for Oliver", asked Malcolm?

"No, no replied Matthew I never thought".

"Ring him there now", said Malcolm, and see if there is any way round this because once this starts it could be a long time before you can access that account again". Matthew rang the bank and asked to be put through to Oliver. He was put straight through and the phone was answered on the first ring. Malcolm left the room to see if Sarah had the letter typed as he walked back in he heard. "

How could I have forgotten to ask you if you needed to take money from that account before I put that request up on the screen?" "Matthew I'm so sorry there is no way around it unless you can contact Claire and get her to come in with you so you can withdraw some money".

"I wouldn't give her the pleasure", said Matthew, "listen Oliver thanks for all your help anyways I'll talk to you bye".

Matthew hung up his head raced ok I'm earning 700 euros a week I definitely have work for the next two months no need to panic yet.

"Are you ok asked Malcolm?"

"I'll be fine", said Matthew; Oliver says there is no way around it so go ahead freeze the assets Claire is fine she has no assets to be frozen to begin with".

"Will you get by", asked Malcolm?

"I'll have to", said Matthew, "but the best thing to do is start the ball rolling as soon as possible the sooner things get underway the better". "The sooner we start the sooner we finish".

For a reason Matthew couldn't explain he started laughing.

"It never rains but it pours excuse me Malcolm I must be loosing it".

"Well said Malcolm it's as well you have the strength in you to sort things out I've seen so many people in your situation fall to pieces and loose everything".

"I've already lost everything", Matthew replied, "everything that matters anyways". Matthew returned home exhausted. Mrs. O'Brien Shelia, Seorsha and the children were playing on the green in front of the houses.

"Matthew you coming to play rounders", asked Shelia.

"Ah thanks I'll give it a miss".

They all looked at one another Matthew went in home and sat on the couch.

"Its finally hit home", said Seorsha.

"Yeah", said Shelia, "we will have to keep a good eye on him for the next few weeks". *That's it so; thought Matthew to himself there's no sense to any of this. It's over now it's obvious I'm never going to get Claire back and I don't even want her anymore.*

As for Dave he may as well never have existed.

Whilst Matthew sat lost in thought he was called back to earth by the phone ringing. It was Justine.

"Matthew I'm just ringing to thank you for the show and for mentioning us so much". "The place was inundated today". "In one day alone I sold six foreign holidays, ten weekend breaks around Ireland of course the fifty euro vouchers helped to". "Matthew this means so much to me I had a none to pleasant visit with the bank manager but if business starts to take off we could be ok".

"Your welcome Justine", "I'm glad something good could come out of this". "Listen I'm glad to hear from you and all but I'm going to go now".

"Matthew", said Justine, "are you having a bad day you seem a bit down".

"Look Justine it was lovely of you to call and all but I really don't want to talk right now".

"Matthew said Justine I was wondering would you come out to dinner with me some night a treat just to say thanks".

"That would be nice", said Matthew, "get back to me on it I'm exhausted now Justine I can't talk anymore thanks for ringing I'm away".

Matthew hung up. Matthew went out and got into the car the estate was quiet not a soul in sight. He drove down to the off license and got a bottle of wine. He drove back up home parked the car and got out he turned his key in the door opened it and left the keys hanging in the lock on the outside of the door. He went into the sitting room and left down the bottle of wine on the coffee table. He went upstairs showered shaved put on a sweat pants and t-shirt. He went back into the bathroom and brushed his teeth with the last of the toothpaste in the tube. He opened the press above the sink where they kept extras of everything Claire was so organized they never ran out of anything. There on the shelf beside the toothpaste he saw them Zimovane 7.5mgs Claire's sleeping tablets. *It must have been a guilty conscience that stopped her sleeping thought Matthew.*

And then it swept over him a thought a resigned thought that all was lost that nothing mattered and that the best he could do was rest in the peaceful earth for eternity. The calm cold clay seemed inviting even comforting. He never bothered to take the extra tube of toothpaste from the shelf instead he took the sleeping tablets from the shelf and put them in his pocket and went down stairs. Matthew went into the sitting room turned on the television put a fire log in the grate and lit it and surrounded it with coal. It was then he noticed he had no glass for the bottle of wine that sat on the table in the off license bag. He took the bottle out with him and opened it with a pop. He returned to the sitting room with the glass and bottle of wine the fire blazed pleasantly in the background there were ads on the television. Matthew took the remote control from the mantle piece went over to the recliner sat in it and kicked out the bottom and took the box of zimovane from his pocked. He had never planned to do this but the decision to do this gave him a great feeling of peace and inner calm. Even though he was determined that this was to be his last night on earth he had no feelings of regret or despair he felt relief as if a great weight had been lifted from him, and he smiled. Matthew poured himself out a large glass of wine. He looked up at the television screen the ads had ended and now "My name is Earl" followed by friends so don't go anywhere a voice said. Matthew took two tablets from the packet of sleeping tablets and swallowed them with a large swig of wine. "You know that guy that goes into the store at ten in the morning for a dutchy and a packet of cigarettes, the guy you wait to come out before you and your family go in, that's me". This caught Matthew's attention he knocked back what was left in his glass of wine and poured himself another glass. He watched as Earl scratched his lottery ticket, as he got knocked down. Then suddenly it was like his eye lids weighed a ton and despite himself they closed. As Earl discovered Karma Matthew was launched into the deepest sleep he had, had in a long time. He turned onto his side in his sleep and the packet of zimovane fell to the floor from his lap underneath the recliner chair.

Justine had a bad feeling since she hung up the phone to Matthew. It was ten o clock she picked up her car keys from the kitchen counter. She looked around the apartment her partner sitting in the armchair in front of the television asleep in a drunken stupor as usual and Yvonne in her room listening to her music. Before she left she went into Yvonne's room.

"For gods sake Yvonne keep your headphones on don't wake him".

"Why where are you going?"

"I'm worried about Matthew I rang him there not so long ago and he is very down I wont be long I just want to see he is ok".

"Grand", said Yvonne.

Justine drove to the shop on the way she always worried that she had forgotten to turn on the alarm, she got back in the car and drove to number eleven the new estate. Eleven at last she said and her jaw dropped she was right something was wrong Matthew's keys were in the outside of the door. She got out of the car and walked up the drive to the door. Then she hesitated turned around and walked away she went up to the next door neighbors door and knocked. Mrs. O'Brien answered the door with Hanna in her arms. "I'm sorry for knocking your door so late". Hanna was crying.

"I hope I didn't wake her", said Justine.

"No", said Mrs. O'Brien, she's teething mad at the minute.

"Hi I'm Justine do you remember me, she said to Hanna. "I'm worried about Matthew I was talking to him earlier and he seemed very down".

"Yeah", said Mrs. O'Brien, "we noticed that today to".

"That's his house isn't it?" Justine asked.

"Yeah that's it", said Mrs. O'Brien.

"I think there is something wrong, said Justine the keys are on the outside of the door". "Well they were not there when we were coming in from the green at half seven and I never noticed him going out that's not to say he didn't".

Mrs. O'Brien bounced Hanna up and down on her hip.

"Here she said to Justine can you take her for me for a minute come in come in I'll just ring Shelia".

The minute Justine took Hanna in her arms she stopped crying.

"Ah", said Mrs. O'Brien you have the charm.

"She's in shock said Justine she's sizing me up give her a minute and she will be off again".

Shelia picked up her phone "hello?"

"Hello", Shelia it's me are you in bed?

"No Perpetual I'm up I'm watching television why?"

"Seems there could be something wrong at Matthew's the keys in the outside of the door and Justine your one who sold him the cruise is here she was talking with him she has a bad feeling since".

"One minute said Shelia me and Seorsha will meet you out front".

Shelia hung up.

"Right", said Mrs. O'Brien we'll meet them out front come on.

Justine went to hand Hanna back to Mrs. O'Brien.

"Your ok love she's grand and settled there I'll just grab her a blanket Mrs. O'Brien handed the blanket to Justine she's grand and settled with you, you carry her you're a natural".

They walked out the drive and met up with Shelia. Seorsha stood at the door ringing the bell.

"No answer", he said, ye wait here, I'll go in God knows what's facing us inside. Seorsha turned the handle and took the keys from the door in with him. When he walked into the hall he heard the television. Oh he thought he must be in the sitting room. He opened the sitting room door and noticed the fire blazing away pleasantly in the grate, then he heard a noise that made him jump followed by a large snort. Seorsha began to laugh Matthew was asleep on the recliner snoring. He walked out to the front door.

"Come on in its all ok he's asleep on the chair in front of the television".

Justine carrying Hanna, Shelia and Mrs. O'Brien walked in. Mrs. O'Brien walked over to the chair where Matthew was sleeping and picked up the half empty bottle of wine. "Drowning his sorrow and no harm either".

Shelia took a throw from the couch and threw it over him. Seorsha took the fireguard and put it in front of the fire. They all turned to leave Seorsha still had the keys in his hand he locked the door from the outside and threw the keys back in through the letterbox.

"I'm so sorry for dragging you all out on a wild goose chase", said Justine.

"Not at all", said Mrs. O'Brien.

"Yeah", said Shelia better to be safe than sorry.

"You did the right thing", said Seorsha.

"Come on", said Mrs. O'Brien we'll go into mine for a cup of tea.

Justine turned to Seorsha and handed him Hanna.

"You to Justine", said Mrs. O'Brien.

"Thanks very much", said Justine, "but I better be getting back".

"Some other time maybe", said Mrs. O'Brien, "you'd be more than welcome".

"Thanks", said Justine, "I'd like that", she got back in her car and drove home.

Justine pulled up in the car parking space outside the apartment she could see the light was off in Yvonne's room. She turned the key and walked up the stairs and into the living room. Tony sat pretending to be asleep on the chair when Claire came in he was drunk again. Justine went over to Yvonne's bedroom she pushed open the door she wasn't there.

"Where's Yvonne", Tony she asked.

He kept talking a load of incomprehensible rubbish.

What does it matter thought Justine let her off probably better not to know.

Emmet heard banging at his door, he opened it.

"What's all this?" he asked.

"Can I stay the night with you?" asked Yvonne.

"Won't your mother be wondering where you are?"

" I doubt that she's not there anyways".

"Okay", said Emmet, "but you've got to sleep on the couch".

"That's fine by me", said Yvonne.

Emmet went upstairs get Yvonne some blankets and a pillow.

"I've no bed for the spare room I keep meaning to get one, would you have some hot chocolate".

"There's no need", said Yvonne, "I'm grand".

Emmet said "I'll let you get to sleep so"

Yvonne lay down on the sofa to sleep as Emmet left the room he looked back she looked so small, and so pale and so angry.

He went up to bed and slept. He got up at eight the next morning he thought he and Yvonne would go to The dinners delight for their breakfast. The clothes were folded neatly at the bottom of the couch a piece of paper lay on top of them.

Thanks for letting me stay xx.

Emmet took the blankets upstairs and put them back in the hot press, he had a shower and got dressed. Before he left for work at 9.45 am he rang Yvonne.

"Hello", she answered.

"You were up and gone early", said Emmet.

"Yeah", said Yvonne thanks again see you Saturday.

"Are you ok Yvonne", asked Emmet?

"Yeah course I am see you Saturday".

"Ok so see you Saturday", said Emmet.

Dave left Claire at the breakfast table. He felt bad over what had happened what was wrong with him, his best friend in the world how had this happened. Yet he couldn't hide the grin of satisfaction that was constantly on display these days.

What's wrong with me thought Dave.

Ah well he thought I'm not all the bad or else I wouldn't be feeling so guilty. Dave hated that he had to go to Matthew asking for money time and time again, but delighted in the fact that Matthew was a soft touch and that he would never ask him to pay the money back. Dave knew he had and was now shitting on Matthew from a height. He knew he was doing it but he couldn't help himself it's not all my fault he told himself Matthew should grow a pair like who wouldn't take advantage when it's so easy? One time it had seemed like Matthew was copping on it seemed like the well was running dry. Dave had rung Matthew up said he needed three hundred euros or he was in deep trouble he could be shot.

"Is that so Matthew" had said, "look we are very busy down here on the site best of luck with raising that money it shouldn't be too hard you're a bookie get a tip off one of your customers".

Matthew had hung up. Dave was distraught he wanted to go to London for the weekend, and he was broke he had lost two thousand in three days at the Galway races He closed up shop and went down to the local casualty complaining of tightness in his chest. Once he was admitted to a ward and had a heart monitor fitted he rang Matthew.

"Matthew its Dave I'm in the hospital I got chest pain they think I probably have had a heart attack". "They have this monitor on me they think stress brought it on".

Matthew rushed down to the hospital on the way to the ward he took out three hundred euros.

"Dave I got here as soon as I could here's the money it might help take away some of the stress". "Oh my God you poor thing what's those wires on you?"

"Oh, said Dave it's telemetry in case I have another heart attach".

"This is a nice ward, said Matthew is it new".

"Yeah", said Dave "it's the medical day ward".

"This is terrible", said Matthew, "you should be in ICU or some special ward believe me Dave I know I watch ER this is a terrible state of affairs I'll get on to someone about this I'll be back with you in a minute".

"No, no Matthew said Dave don't go making a fuss I'm sure that they know what they are doing".

"Alright Dave", Matthew had said, "don't be getting upset it's not good for you I won't say anything if you don't want me to".

That evening the doctors did their rounds.

"Mr. Danaher, the doctor said it's good news your trop t is normal both your ecg's are normal". "We will let you go home and to be on the safe side we will bring you in on Monday for a stress test but we are sure it's nothing to worry about".

Dave packed his bags the nurse removed the needle from his arm and he went out to the car park got in his car and drove to Shannon airport he had his bag already packed in the boot, he had his tickets and passport in his wallet and three hundred euros spending money in his pocket good old reliable Matthew. As Dave was standing in line at the gate waiting to board the plane Matthew rang.

"Hello", said Dave, "how are you?.

"More to the point", said Matthew, "how are you I rang the hospital and they said they discharged you".

"Yeah", said Dave. "they had no beds so they sent me home I'm going back Monday for a stress test it was a heart attack alright".

"This is scandalous", said Matthew, "are you at home I'm driving over there right now and taking you to another hospital one with beds".

"I'm on the tablets Matthew there is nothing else they can do for me". "I'm going to spend the weekend in bed", so I am resting.

"I'll come over and see you".

"No Matthew there is no need look I appreciate it but I want to be alone it was a shock to get and I want some alone time to take it in reflect ya know". "

Ok, said Matthew but if you get the slightest twinge you ring me do you hear, promise me now".

"I will Matthew don't be worrying".

This is the final call...

"What's that Dave", Matthew asked.

"The television I'm watching some film about a fellow in an airport".

"Oh right said Matthew".

"Look", Matthew, said Dave, "I want to get some rest".

"Oh I'm sorry said Matthew you must be wrecked I'll let you go and remember this the slightest twinge and you ring me".

"I will do Matthew", said Dave, "thanks you're a great friend".

Dave smiled away to him self as he remembered it that was classic, Dave thought to himself even if I do say so myself. Ah but not as good as the time he gave me three thousand to pay off the crime family whose car I crashed into Dave laughed. He had wanted three thousand for the holding deposit on the apartment he was now living in problem was that he didn't have it. He knew that if he told Matthew what it was really for he would have to give it back because Matthew would know that he would be getting it back. So what did he do he invented his very own crime family names and occupations for all eight of them, from dog breeding to gun running.

"Oh a terrible crew to be mixed up with", he had told Matthew terrible. "See I was driving in the road and the sun was in my eyes and I drove straight across the junction not seeing that I was at the junction".

"Oh Matthew it was terrible they swivered to avoid me my car was untouched but they went straight into a wall at the other side of the road". "Straight away they rang the others there must have been thirty of them there". "They told me not to call the guards and I was afraid to so I just stood there alone amongst them".

"Jesus, said Matthew you must have been terrified".

"Ah no, said Dave I'm used to scum like that but I wouldn't be stupid enough to call the guards or god knows what they would do". "I wouldn't be scared for myself but for you and Claire all my friends because they would know I would be well able for them so they would go after you my friends". "I was thinking of you all ye and yer safety was all that was going through my head".

"God Dave and you in such danger and all you were thinking of was us", said Matthew. "Well, said Dave it's in times of danger like that that your priorities become clear".

"I suppose it is Dave", said Matthew, "but I think I'd be selfish I'd only be thinking of me and my safety".

"Well, said Dave I don't know what you would do but that was my reaction". "We want three thousand by tomorrow morning they said for the damage to our car"." Alright I said I have to meet them in the car park tomorrow at seven in the morning". "I haven't got the money I guess I'll just have to go down there in the morning and face them".

"Go to the Guards", said Matthew.

"Like I explained earlier they know they can't mess with me but I'd be afraid they would go after my friends".

"Don't worry about us Matthew had said go to the guards tell them your story, look after yourself".

"No I wouldn't have what could happen you and Claire on my conscience it would just be selfish of me to protect myself and leave you both in danger no, no I wont go to the guards I'll just go down there in the morning face the music like a man".

"You will not be going down there with no money if you're adamant to do this I'll give you the money and I'll come down with you, you're not doing this alone".

"No", Dave had said, "I'm doing this to protect both you and Claire I can't have you coming down with me incase something happens you then all this would be worthless". "Fine, said Matthew, there's no talking to you, you do what you think is best but I'm coming straight over and you'll take the money and that's the end of it".

"Ok? Right so, said Dave if you insist I'll take the money but you'll stay at home safe in the morning I won't have you risk your safety around people like that".

The following morning at ten o clock when the estate agents opened Dave took Matthews money and put down the holding deposit on his apartment. When Matthew had heard Dave was buying an apartment he had insisted on giving him the deposit. Without a twinge of guilt Dave accepted.

I'm a fucking legend Dave thought to himself, I should write a book my memoirs ah well a fool and their money are easily parted, sometimes my stories are so good that I believe them myself.

Dave threw back his head and laughed. Whilst Dave was well aware of the price of everything he could appreciate the value of nothing. The fact that he had just lost the best friend he ever had didn't cost him a thought. How will I manage now he thought without access to Matthew's purse strings? He smiled to himself yeah that's right I took his purse so Ill be fine. I'd love to see the look on his face when he finds out we've cleaned him out. Yet Dave couldn't shake the pangs of guilt he felt from time to time no matter how hard he tried to ignore them. Dave knew half the money wasn't Claire's she only worked two days a week, but then again like she said she was his wife she was entitled to half.

Well thought Dave it's really nothing to do with me it's between the two of them. It's not *my fault Claire left him either if she had been happy this would never have happened in the first place.*

Dave turned the key in the ignition of his car and reversed out of the car parking space. We'll have to move get a bigger place. Dave's apartment was lovely and all but it was only one bed roomed and they needed at least a second bed room. If it was only to house all those designer clothes Claire has.

Dave thought of the room full of Claire's shoe's handbags and clothes that Matthew had bought her. I wonder what I'd make on eBay for those, thought Dave.

Matthew woke up on the chair his mobile was ringing he eventually found it; it was down the side of the chair. You have three voice mail messages the screen told him. He dialed 171 and listened.

See you, you asshole I want my stuff back now. I'll have Dave have you done he has connections you know. Came booming down the phone to him

Matthew burst out laughing yeah his connected alright but the wiring is loose. Fuck you sunshine. Matthew thought about smashing everything of Claire's to bits cutting all her clothes to ribbons breaking all the heels off her shoes then putting them in a taxi and sending them to her. Then no he thought I won't be sucked into their stupid mindless games. I'm better than that. He packed all Claire's stuff down to the last clip put them in black bags and boxes. He called a taxi he didn't want to ask Seorsha it wasn't fair to drag him into this. The taxi pulled up outside, and Matthew helped the driver who he only knew to see load the stuff.

"Thanks so much for doing this for me".

"Your more than welcome", said the driver. He gave him the address.

"Do you know where that is?"

"Oh I do I know that creepy slimy suffering bejaysus well". "How you ever had anything to do with him is beyond me... yach". "I would have been out of there a long time ago".

"You would have been right", said Mathew.

As the taxi drove away full of Claire's stuff Matthew felt as though a weight had been lifted. The fucking cheek of the bitch though, how dare she, she has no reason to treat me like this what did I ever do to her. Some people are of no benefit to the earth they are just a waste of oxygen. Well fuck her may all bad luck go with her. Dave turned up the street and parked outside the betting office he owned. He noticed there was a car pulled up outside and two men in suits waited outside the door.

That's strange Dave thought.

He got out of the car and walked to the door and inserted the key in the lock of the metal shutter. One of the men turned to Dave.

"Are you Dave Danaher?"

"Yes", said Dave can I help you?

"We will come inside with you for a chat, said the other man".

"So what's this about?" asked Dave.

"Just open the shutter, the man said, and we will go inside for a chat".

Dave turned the key in the shutter and it opened slowly, he then turned the key in the glass door that opened into the shop. He walked in and pushed the door shut full force. Next Dave shoved the key in the lock and tried to hurriedly lock the door. Dave shook so much that he dropped the keys from his hand to the floor. Dave bent down to pick up the keys the two men coming behind him didn't see him and with ease pushed the door open against Dave sending him running backwards arms beating like wings in circles trying to keep his balance in a half sitting half standing posture. He looked just like the neandertol man as he accelerated backwards. For a second it seemed all was not lost Dave pushed himself to an almost standing position and grabbed for a surface to steady himself. But despite his best efforts Dave kept flying backwards finally coming to a stop when he hopped his head off the upright edge of the open counter, splitting his head open and causing him to fall forward busting his nose of the floor.

"Don't hurt me don't hurt me", Dave cried as he curled into a ball on the floor.

"Mr. Danaher really said one of the men we have had all types of reactions from people who do not have a television license but this has to be the most exaggerated reaction ever encountered".

The other man handed him a tissue.

"Sit up here pinch the bridge of your nose and the blood will stop in a minute".

"Here", said the other man, show us the back of your head not too bad but maybe you should go to the hospital and get checked out in case you have concussion or something. The men looked to one another then one man turned to Dave.

"We will be back tomorrow count yourself lucky you fell or you'd be facing a hefty fine and possible jail time have a television license tomorrow".

The two men left. Dave decided that the shock of it all was enough for him for one day he picked up his keys and walked out the door locked the shutter got in his car and drove to the nearest pub for a few half ones to calm his nerves. Claire looked through her purse in delight she decided the best thing to do was have her nails done. There was nothing she wanted now that she couldn't have for today anyway. Just then the buzzer went in the apartment.

"Hello who is it?" Claire asked.

"I'm a taxi driver", came the reply, "Matthew has sent over all your stuff".

"Fine Claire replied bring it on up".

"Away and shite", replied the taxi driver, "what do you think I am a courier service if you want your stuff you'll come down and get it yourself".

"The cheek", said Claire, "you need not think I'm paying you for service like that".

"I've already been paid".

The taxi man took his finger off the buzzer and threw all the bags from the taxi and then put the boxes beside them. He was driving away when Claire emerged from the front door. Claire checked the pigeon hole in the hall where the letters were kept she was surprised to see a letter addressed to herself. Claire looked at the amount of stuff the taxi man had delivered. There is no way I'm carrying all that stuff up all them stairs Dave will have to come home to do it thought Claire. She took out her mobile and phoned the bookies but the number kept ringing out. There were two teenagers kicking a ball off the gable end of the building.

"Hey you two do ye want to earn 20 euros each".

"Yeah", said one.

"Na", said the other, "you're alright Mrs".

"Yeah", said the other then, "you're alright".

"Ok", said Claire, "how about 30 euros".

The teenagers walked over and began to feel the weight of the bags.

"Are you up many floors".

"Three", said Claire we're at the top.

"Oh well then Mrs"., said one of the boys, "I'd say that would cost you 50 euros each that will take us a half hour or more and we don't unpack".

"40 euros," said Claire.

"55", said one of the boys.

"45," said Claire.

"60", said the other boy.

"50", said Claire.

"Right you be, said both the boys 50 it is".

Claire groaned. "Right, said one of the boy's money first".

Claire handed them 50 euros each and they began to carry the bags upstairs. Twenty minutes later and the living room looked like a tip head with all the bin bags. Claire sat at the table took the letter addressed to her from her pocket and read it. It was from the solicitors.

Matthew you fool thought Claire it's a bit late to freeze the account now.

Claire looked for nice clothes it wasn't hard Matthew had labeled all the bags. Claire opened the bag marked boots and pulled out a pair of snow boots. Next she tore open the bag marked jeans and finally she pulled a jumper from the bag marked jumpers. Twenty minutes later Claire was walking out the door of the apartment to the beauticians. I'll get Dave to unpack all that stuff when he comes home I couldn't be bothered. Half an hour after that Claire was walking up the street admiring her nails. As she walked up the street towards home the colorful drawings on a building caught her eye. Travels, she looked up and read the sign. She looked at the different brochures in the window of sandy beaches and sun. And then she saw it New York weekend break 550 euros including taxes and charges. I always wanted to go to New York maybe me and Dave should head to the big apple a break away from here would do us the world of good. Claire walked in the door of the travel agents and sat at one of the chairs in front of the counter. There seemed to be only one girl behind the counter and she was on the phone talking to someone about some ridiculous radio program.

"Excuse me", said Claire, "you might get off the phone and serve me before I have to get on the phone to whoever owns this pathetic little excuse of a travel agents".

"That would be me", said Justine.

"What would be you?" Claire asked.

"The owner of this pathetic travel agents that's who", said Justine.

Justine's temper boiled but she bit her tongue and walked over to Claire smiling. She wasn't going to lose a customer.

"Sorry to have kept you waiting", said Justine, "how can I help you?"

"I'd like to book tickets on a flight to New York for tomorrow or the next day", said Claire for two weeks.

"Ok", said Justine. "Do you want me to book you accommodation too?"

"No", said Claire, "that won't be necessary".

Justine had lost count of how many sales she'd made since that radio show.

"I'd like to fly first class", said Claire, "none of your squashed sardine seating thank you".

"Ok", said Justine, "typing away into the computer".

"Ok I have flights tomorrow leaving Shannon at 22.00 hrs two tickets first class 1,500 each". "Is that of interest to you?" Justine asked.

"It will do I suppose", replied Claire.

"Right names and I'll go ahead and book this for you".

"Claire Ryan, Dave Danaher". "Dave will be delighted when I tell him I've booked us this".

"Oh", said Justine, that's sweet of you your husband, will definitely be surprised.

"That he will", said Claire, "I have given him quiet a few surprises lately, and I still have quiet a good few surprises up my sleeve".

What a strange thing to say thought Justine as she printed off the details; well a sale is a sale. Justine returned from the printer with the flight details and sat down to go through the itinerary with Claire.

"Oh don't bother with that", said Claire; "it's all on the printout isn't it?"

"Yes it is", replied Justine. "If you like I can highlight the departure and return times and that".

"Your fine", said Claire, "I don't know what kind of simpleton usually flies with you I'm perfectly capable of reading a flight schedule".

Claire reached forward and snatched the itinerary from Justine's hand, stood up and turned to leave when she was as far as the door Justine stopped her.

"Excuse me mam", said Justine, "developing a cramp in her face from the forced smile you've forgotten to pay don't worry it's easy forget something when you're in a hurry". "Oh right", said Claire, "how much do I owe you?"

"Three thousand euros", said Justine.

Claire opened her bulging purse Justine thought she would collapse she had never seen so much money before in one persons possession.

"Here", said Claire, as she counted out three thousand euros into Justine's hand.

"I thought I'd spend some of it, said Claire so I could close my purse".

Justine laughed, "we all have our own problems wouldn't do if the stitching in you purse burst". "Hold on and I'll give you a receipt".

Justine put the cash in the till and brought a receipt back to Claire. Claire turned on her heel without saying goodbye or thank you and left. When Claire got home she sat at the table and read over the solicitor's letter again. She felt sorry for poor boring Matthew, and who on earth was advising him. Freezing the account would make life difficult for no one but himself. How will he live? She got a pen and paper and began to write.

To whom it may concern,

I Claire Ryan no longer whish to have any access to any of my ex husbands assets or accounts. Please inform him of same and remove my name from the bank account. I will contact the bank confirming this, and am willing to take any other actions necessary to make these changes. Please tell my husband I am sorry and I whish him all the best for the future.

Yours truly

Claire Ryan.

Claire put on her Jacket and went down to the bank. She went to customer services and removed her name from their accounts. She handed the wallet with the bank and credit cards to the girl behind the counter who said she would have them forwarded to Matthew. She went to the post office and posted her letter to the solicitor's office whose name was at the top of the letter she had received. Claire stopped at cakes and things for a cup of tea and a cream bun on her way home. She felt all happy and excited inside it was as if giving back the bank cards had freed her to start her new life with Dave. Claire smiled all the way as she walked back to the apartment. She couldn't wait for Dave to come home to surprise him. She sat and watched television over the top of the many black plastic bags as she waited for Dave to come home.

7

Dave walked into the bar; everyone turned to look and then turned away again.

"Had to close up for the day", said Dave addressing no one yet any one who would listen.

"Was set upon by two thugs but I was well able for them". "Trying to run a protection racket they were". "Trying to get me to pay protection money to prevent any harm coming to my premises". "I was well able for them though knocked the biggest one out with a punch". "Told the other fella who I was told him my connections they both got up and ran out I won't be hearing from them again in a hurry so I won't". "Told them I'd have them shot". "Give us a swift one there Simon will you a powers".

Simon turned around to the optic and rolled his eyes at the customer at the end of the bar. He turned around and placed the drink on a beer matt in front of Dave. Another customer came in and sat down beside Dave Simon came over to serve him.

"Jesus", Dave he said, "you should head over to the hospital to get checked out your eyes have swollen up loads since you came in here". "They could close up and you won't be able to see a thing". "Are you very sore?"

"Ah no", said Dave, "it's nothing the whiskey can't take care of, give us another half one".

Simon put on a pint of Guinness for the other man and while it settled he handed Dave his half one. Dave knocked it back.

"Call us a taxi will you Simon", asked Dave, "I'm going to head home to bed for the day". "I'll be right as rain when I wake up".

"Not a bother Dave", replied Simon, "straight away".

Three girls walked in the door with bags of shopping.

"Ah a girls day out is it"? Simon called to them as they walked in the door and settled themselves at the bar.

"Can we have three soups and brown bread please", asked Yvonne. "No we weren't shopping its spot prizes for the charity fashion show were putting on in school for St. Vincent de Paul".

"Oh right", said Simon. "So ye are all in transition year so?"

"Yeah", Yvonne replied. "Can we have three cokes", asked Angela?

"Oh make mine a club orange", said Angela.

"Oh two Angela's, what are the odds", asked Simon.

Dave was in deep conversation with the man who sat beside him. Simon frowned as he overheard the conversation.

"So I'll have ye shot in a minute if ye are not away out of here, I said to them".

"Jaysus", the man replied, "you're a fare brave man". "I'd have had a heart attack".

"No, no not me", Dave replied. "Because like I can have anyone I want shot I'm related to everyone if you know what I'm talking about".

Simon slammed the door of the fridge shut.

"Right you", he said to Dave. "That's enough". "Nobody in here wants to hear that bullshit ok?"

Just then Seorsha walked in the door.

"Hi Simon, I believe you have a fare for me".

"Here", said Simon pointing at Dave who turned around in the stool.

"Ah", said Seorsha, "I see you got your just deserts, and no harm either". "That explains why your shut so and to think that I thought you had developed a conscience, and had the common decency not to show your face".

Seorsha turned to Simon. "Sorry there mate but I won't be able to take that fare for you".

"Do you know who that is?"

"That's the man who ran away with Matthew Ryan's wife".

"Excuse me a minute", said Dave. "My personal life is none of your business and you can't refuse to take me because of it".

"That's where your wrong said Seorsha". "My car my rules my choice". "Hi Yvonne, you needn't be hiding in the corner there at all I can see you".

"Hi Seorsha I'm not hiding we got a half day to organize spot prizes for the fashion show". "Could you ask Matthew if he is still on for doing it?" "It's ok if he doesn't feel like it it's only natural after what's his been through". "But we need to know because we will have to find someone else".

"I'll ask him this evening when I get home".

Dave banged his glass of the counter, another Simon.

"You've had enough", said Simon.

"I'll be the judge of that", said Dave.

"Right", said Simon, "out you go you look a sight and you're frightening my customers with your stupid wankster talk out, out your barred".

Dave picked up the empty glass and smashed it off the floor. With blood dripping down from his nose Dave staggered from the bar towards home.

Having got rid of everything Claire owned from the house Matthew began to clean. For some strange reason he felt great. He had all upstairs done. He decided to begin downstairs with the sitting room. He picked up the wine bottle and kicked in the open recliner and there they were the zimovane. I can't even kill myself right he thought. I'm some prize fool that I would do that to myself over the likes of her when I have so much to live for. And live I will from here on out. Matthew looked up at the clock it was six o clock. I never felt that time going he looked around in satisfaction the place was shining. Once a week should be enough to keep the place right.

The door bell rang. "Come in", Matthew shouted.

Mrs. O'Brien and Shelia walked in.

"Hi" Matthew. He walked to the door of the sitting room and they spoke in the hall. "Where are the children?" Matthew asked.

"They are with Seorsha". "You had a great sleep last night in that chair there", said Shelia.

Matthew blushed.

"Don't be embarrassed son", said Mrs. O'Brien, "we're all entitled to feel sorry for ourselves by times".

"Yeah", said Shelia, "but mind yourself that getting drunk in front of the fire doesn't become a habit".

"It won't", said Matthew, "I promise".

"And what's more Matthew", said Mrs. O'Brien, "at the risk of sounding harsh you need to cop your self on and stop wallowing, no more Greta Garbo impersonations". "Yeah", I agree said Shelia.

"Matthew look around you", Mrs. O'Brien continued, "look at poor Billy his wife in hospital no knowing what's ahead of them". "Look at all the people around you what happened you is terrible don't get me wrong but at the end of the day no one died and you can do so much better for yourself. Don't let this one bad terrible experience define you".

"I won't", said Matthew, "I was thinking the same myself all day".

"You'll never guess who was over here last night worried about you", said Mrs. O'Brien?

"Who?" Matthew asked.

They were both relieved a few days ago the immediate reply would have been Claire. "Wait", said Matthew, "let's all sit down and be comfortable".

They went into the sitting room and sat down. Matthew threw a fire log into the fire and lit it.

"Now what will ye have tea, coffee, wine??"

"Oh go on", said Shelia, "we will have wine".

The three of them sat down to chat glass of wine in hand.

"Right", said Matthew, "shoot who was here last night?"

"Justine", replied Shelia.

"She had a bad feeling about you after getting off the phone to you and decided to call over to see you were ok".

"And good thing", said Mrs. O'Brien, "because you left the door and car keys in the outside of the door".

"Yeah", said Shelia, "only for Justine you could have woken up this morning dead with your car stolen".

"And", said Mrs. O'Brien, "you were in here asleep in a chair drunk with no spark guard in front of the fire, you could have been burnt to death". "What are we going to do with you?"

"I promise you ladies there is no need to worry about me". "Today I woke up on that chair to voice mails from Claire threatening me harm if she didn't get her clothes immediately". "And something clicked". "I'm glad she's gone I'm better off without her; she never gave a shit about me". "And as for that wankster Dave what a fool why was I ever even friends with him, I ask myself". "No I loaded her stuff into a taxi and it was the best feeling ever like a weight had been lifted". "The three years with Claire were never enjoyable only stressful nothing was good enough for her". "I gave her everything she wanted and still it wasn't enough". "From the time I met her I was doing all I could to make myself good enough for her and today I realized ,and I hope you don't think I'm full of myself or anything, that Claire was never good enough for me". "I'm going starting fresh".

"You should go thank Justine", said Mrs. O'Brien.

"I intend to", said Matthew, "first thing in the morning".

Dave staggered upstairs feeling dizzy. Claire ran over to him. "What happened you Dave are you ok?"

"Yeah", said Dave, "I'm fine a bit sore that's all but you should see the other guy Claire". "They came into the shop two of them". "Huge they were trying to start up a protection racket". "I wasn't long running them let me tell you". "They won't be back". "I've a surprise for us", said Claire,"you won't believe this it was really spur of the moment".

"I could do with a surprise", said Dave, "after the day I had".

"I went into the pub for a swift one for the pain after I beat up those goons and I asked to be called a taxi". "Seorsha came and refused to carry me honestly I have enough of this town". "I'd love to pack up and go everyone is into everyone's business here".

"Me too", said Claire, "and you know what Dave it might just be possible". "I got us two tickets to New York today". "For tomorrow can you believe?"

Dave jumped up and threw his arms around Claire.

"This is just what we need a fresh start you're the best Claire". "I could sell the bookies we could get an apartment there everything will be great".

"We're flying first class", said Claire. "This is just what we need we're not the type of people for a small minded place like this".

"Your right said Dave and we can apply for a green card from over there".

"We leave tomorrow night at ten o clock".

"Right", said Dave, "where are we staying?"

"We're staying at the Gramercy Park Hotel oh Dave wait until you hear about it'. "I just booked it on line the web site says "the lobby is a rhapsody of "Haute Bohemian" chic and Renaissance opulence". "Oh Dave I can't wait'. "I booked us in for two weeks it's expensive mind 7,000 euros for the fortnight but we deserve it". "This is just the start we need to a new life in a new country". "We'll never look back Dave, never".

"Oh I know Claire I'm so sorry for what I did Matthew he was a great friend but from the moment I saw you I knew you were the only one for me". "I'm sorry that we hurt Matthew but I know everything will be okay now; we are meant for each other". "We deserve our happiness and a fresh start".

"Yeah", said Claire, "I have a good feeling about this I think we are doing the right thing". "I think everything is going to be ok".

"Right", said Claire, "we have to make a list if we have our minds definitely made up to leave here and never come back we have to decide what to take and what to leave behind". "I'll need to take all my clothes actually so I am going to get big boxes and post on all my stuff swift post to the hotel it will arrive before the two weeks are up and I'm sure in that time we will find an apartment".

"That's a good idea", said Dave, "I have boxes like wardrobes for clothes that I bought on line for packing when I moved in here". "They are down stairs in the basement". "I'll go down and get them". "There is five of them I'll only need two you can take three". "Let's agree apart from clothing we won't take anything with us deal". "No trinkets from our past lives we are starting anew".

"Ok". "Fine by me", said Claire.

Dave went down to the basement and one by one he carried up the folded large boxes. It took Claire and Dave two hours to reassemble the boxes.

"Lets pack tomorrow babe lets go to bed".

"No", said Claire, "we should stay up and do this we are going tomorrow remember?" "We would be better off to stay up and do this and be ready to have them taken tomorrow". "I don't think we will be able to post them we will have to get DHL or someone".

"Look Claire see the state of me I need my rest"." All my clothes are in the wardrobe my shoes are in the bottom on the floor". "You wouldn't be a sweetheart and pack for me?"

" Oh Dave", said Claire, "I got caught up in the moment I'm so sorry I wasn't thinking you go away on to bed I'll pack us".

Dave went to bed and Claire stayed up all night packing both their clothes. At eight am Dave got up.

"Have you not got the breakfast on?" Dave asked.

"Is it that time already", asked Claire, "I'll get something on now what would you like?"

"A fry would be nice?"

"But Dave we've got no fry in the house".

"Guess you'll have to go to the shop so babe". Dave gave Claire a kiss on the lips "I'm away for a shower".

Claire sighed and walked over to the chair she had her coat hanging on put it on and went to the shop for fry. Claire wasn't feeling tired she was too excited imagine tonight at ten o clock is the last I'll ever see of this poxy place, she thought. She came back home from the shop and before she began to fry she called DHL.

"We'll be there before lunch".

"Oh my God that's great", said Claire, "I was so afraid you wouldn't be able to do it, we're leaving at ten tonight and we have no one to organize anything for us".

Dave walked out of the shower feeling refreshed and hungry.

"Claire babe is the breakfast not ready yet?"

"I'm just making it now", said Claire.

"Have you all our stuff packed?"

"Yeah I do", said Claire, "but there's no need for you to thank me".

"Oh is someone grumpy this morning?"

"Well I've been up all night packing our stuff to go live in a foreign country with my money and now I'll go cook our breakfast that I bought as well".

"What did you just say, asked Dave, your money maybe I should call the guards and ask them whose money it is".

Dave picked up the phone.

"Don't, don't said Claire I'm just tired that's all".

"That's more like it", Dave said, "now hurry it up".

Claire went over and took the frying pan from the press and began to cook. Her back was turned to Dave and as she coked the tears ran down her face. Dave walked over to get himself a glass of juice and saw Claire crying.

"Oh babe I'm so sorry are you crying because of me". "I didn't mean it I'm so sore I wouldn't be surprised if my ribs are broken I'm just not able to do anything to help and I feel so bad about seeing you do all this that I'm frustrated".

"It's fine Dave I understand it's not just you it's just so much has happened in the past few days it's a lot to take in".

"Oh, said Dave don't worry I'm sure everything is going to be ok babe once we move we'll be fine, now watch the breakfast we don't want to be eating burned food now do we".

Claire returned to cooking. They ate breakfast and Claire went out to see if there were any children around she could pay to carry out the stuff. Eventually the two children arrived out to kick the ball off the wall.

"Hi boy's", said Claire, something caught her eye it was Dave coming down the stairs maybe he was going to help with the boxes after all.

"I'm away down to the pub for a few babe", said Dave. 'Say goodbye to the lads". "Right", said Claire.

Typical man she thought. The two boys were standing beside her.

"Do you want something moved one of them asked?"

"Yeah", Claire said. "We are moving DHL is coming I need boxes brought down".

"It will cost you 100 euros that missus", said one of the boys.

Claire didn't have the energy to argue she handed over the money and the two boys ran upstairs and between them an hour later just as the DHL van pulled up all the stuff was down stairs. After they were loaded Claire set the alarm for six she hoped to get a little bit of sleep. If they left for seven they would be at Shannon for eight and that would be just right they would be booked in two hours before their flight. Claire rang Dave to make sure he knew they had to leave for seven. She knew she would have to drive Dave wouldn't be drinking water. The phone rang and rang but there was no answer. Claire sent a text.

Hi babe just making sure you remember we need to leave for seven we have to book in two hours before our flight.

Claire fell asleep on the chair she woke up at half five and checked her phone. Dave hadn't texted back. She picked up the phone and rang him. Again it rang and rang with no answer. Claire was getting worried Jesus what if he'd left it was all too much for him she wasn't what he wanted after all. Why had she to argue with him this morning? She was so stupid but she hadn't meant it. She understood that he was sore from dealing with those chancers the previous day. God he was so brave, not like wimpy Matthew he would have pissed himself handed over the money to get rid of them and call the guards. Dave was a real man it was refreshing. It just dawned on Claire they would have to go in the clothes they had on them she had forgotten to leave out clothes for them. Claire left out the receipt for the tickets and the two passports. She left the keys for the apartment on top of them. Six thirty and still there's no Dave what am I going to do? He is gone I've scared him off. Claire rang him again, still no answer. Oh sweet Jesus I know what happened those fuckers from yesterday they caught him and they've beat him up again. What am I going to do? Claire rang the hospital they had no patient Dave Danaher. Should she ring the guards? 6.55 Claire could see Dave walking towards the entrance to their building. He wasn't staggering and showed no signs of being drunk or having been attacked. Thank God, said Claire. Thank God. Claire was worried Dave would be drunk and they would be refused access to the plane. Claire picked up the passports ticket receipt and keys and put them in her bag she then checked to make sure she had her purse she opened it and looked in. All sorted. Dave walked in the door of the apartment.

"I was so worried you'd be late".

"Don't be stressing babe I got your text and what's the story with all the phone calls?"

"I was worried about you that's all".

"Don't be silly babe", he lent into Claire and gave her a kiss.

The sweet smell of woman's perfume greeted Claire. What the fuck, she was about to say but she stopped herself now was not the time.

"Will I leave you on your own for a minute Dave", to say good-bye to the apartment. "Yeah", said Dave that would be nice. "Here are the keys to my car you start it up and I'll meet you out front".

Claire checked her bag again to make sure she had everything in it and then went down stairs started the car and reversed it out of the car parking space and drove it over to the entrance of the building. Dave lifted the loose board from the bottom of the wardrobe and pulled up a metal box and left it on the floor. He then took the hanger bar from the wardrobe and shook it and a key fell out he picked it up turned it in the lock and pulled out a huge wad of money in excess of 300,000 euros. Come to daddy babe come to daddy. He put a bum bag around his waste and shoved the money in it and hid it beneath his clothes. He walked out the door and banged it shut behind him. Claire was pulled up outside the door in the car. He sat in and they drove off. They arrived in Shannon at eight ten. They went to the desk and checked in.

"Have you any luggage to check through?"

"Oh my God Dave we've forgotten to bring any luggage. We've no toothpaste or deodorant or anything".

Dave laughed, "she's a bit of an air head he said to the air-hostess".

"Never mind", she said, "you can buy stuff once you go through to departures just keep in mind 100ml quantities only".

"Thanks", said Claire, and they walked through to the departure gates and through the metal detector.

"We leave through gate C". "I'll just run to the chemist and get some toiletries.

"Get me some too babe won't you".

"I'll get you a toothbrush and toothpaste that's what I'm getting myself we can get everything else over".

"Here", said Dave, "give us some money I'll pay you back once I sell the bookies I'll go over there to the bar and have a pint while you go to the chemist". "It's horrible not having money". "I hate asking you it's only temporary and soon I'll be looking after you". "Dave gave Claire a kiss. "I'll be over there in that bar". "I love you".

Claire laughed, "its cool babe".

Claire gave Dave 50 euros. Claire went to the chemist and bought two toothbrushes and a small toothpaste. She then went back to join Dave at the bar, the time was flying they would be boarding in under an hour.

"Ah here she is now", said Dave to the bar man he was the only one in the bar. "It's the woman of my dreams".

Claire smiled.

"What will you have to drink babe it's on me, said Dave". "I'm an old fashioned guy, Dave said to the bar man I think the man should always pay for his lady".

"Yeah said Claire joking especially if he's paying with your own money I'll have a Bacardi and coke".

"Oh well if you want to be an independent woman don't let me stop you. Like I always say, Dave said to the barman the woman is always right".

"That will be 5 euros 60 cent", the barman said to Claire.

Claire opened her purse.

"And take for a pint for me"; said Dave, "I'm just ready for one".

Claire paid for the two drinks. Could Mrs. Ryan and Mr. Danaher please make their way to gate C for flight EI704 to

New York? Dave and Claire stood up and went to run to the plane the long corridor was deserted. They turned the corner just before their gate Dave caught up to Claire and caught her by the arm squeezing it tight.

"Don't ever do that to me in public again". "How dare you try to embarrass me in public?"

"I don't know what you're talking about", said Claire.

"I'm talking about that stunt you pulled in the bar there saying that".

"I was only joking please stop your hurting me".

This is the last call for Mrs. Ryan and Mr. Danaher boarding flight EI704 to New York. Dave let go of Claire's arm

"I'm so sorry babe I'm just so stressed lately".

"It's ok", said Claire, "it's ok come on and we'll get our flight".

The airhost stood at the desk tapping her wrist.

"We're not obliged to wait for you; you know people have schedules to keep".

She grabbed the passports and took a quick look at them follow me hurry up. They were taken and seated in first class. The seats were so spacious. They reclined right back. When they were seated they were handed menus with a choice of starter main course and desert. The plane began to move along the runway and next they were in the air and all that was before them was new and all that was behind them already seemed distant another existence. Claire flicked through her menu.

Oh my God, oh my God what have I gotten myself into? What have I gotten myself into?

She then heard a noise beside her like a dog whimpering. She turned to see Dave crying. "I'm so sorry. I'm so sorry I didn't mean to do that I swear I'll never hurt you again". "I'll do anything you want me to do". "Anything you just say it".

Claire took a sigh of relief everything was going to be ok.

"It's alright Dave".

"I'm just feeling so guilty over Matthew".

"Its ok", said Claire, "I understand all the pressure your under"." I know you would never do anything like that normally".

"I'll change I'll learn how to channel my anger more positively".

"And I'll help you Dave just let me know what I can do".

"Oh Claire I love you so much and I will do for ever and ever".

Dave put his arm around Claire and she cuddled up to him.

"I love you too Dave more than anyone else in the world ever; I know we are going to be ok". They arrived in New York JFK airport it was Claire's first time in New York. The vastness of JFK airport with its eight terminals amazed her. There was a great buzz with throngs of people coming and going. People running on the little moving pathways designed to save you having to walk. Everyone was in such a big hurry. The atmosphere when they stepped into Jfk convinced Claire and Dave they were doing the right thing. Claire felt so alive and happy surrounded by the bright lights and all the activity around them. They passed through emigration and then walked in a daze behind the other passengers until they realized they were in the baggage hall and they had no bags. They then turned and followed the directions to the arrivals hall. Dave and Claire went to burger king and had two whopper meals. They sat in stunned silence as they watched all the activity around them. When they had finished without a word Dave got up and took the two trays and emptied them into the bin. When he came back to the table he took Claire's hands in his.

"We're here babe everything is going to be great I can feel it".

Claire's face lit up with joy she couldn't remember the last time she had felt this happy if ever. When they went to the exit there were men holding up cards to drive people to their destinations. Claire and Dave were amazed to see their names being held up.

"It has to be a coincidence", Dave said to Claire.

"Yeah", said Claire, imagine and they both burst out laughing.

Just then the man called out Danaher and Ryan for the Gramercy Park Hotel. Oh my God they said in unison. Dave caught Claire by the hand.

"Babe, babe its for us", and they both began to run towards the man.

"Are you Ryan and Danaher", the driver asked?

"Yeah", said Claire.

"I'm Shawn your driver". "Please follow me". "Where are your bags?" the man asked. "Oh", said Matthew, "we came over here to shop so what we have on us is enough".

"Ha, ha", the man laughed, "good enough".

They followed him out to a black escalade. There were two cocktails waiting for them on flip out tables in front of their seat.

"So where are you from?" The driver asked.

"We are Irish", said Claire.

"Yeah", said Matthew, "a small town called Nenagh bet you never heard of it".

"Your going to be amazed", said the driver, "but I have heard of it and do you want to know how?"

"Yeah", said Claire sipping on the two straws in her lovely blue colored cocktail.

"My Grandfather was from Toomevara it's a small village outside Nenagh are you both familiar with it?"

"Yeah, yeah we are", said Claire. "I don't want to be rude or anything but how?" "You don't look a bit Irish".

"My Grandmother was from Haiti". "They met when the Toomevara GAA club went on their holiday there after winning the Dan Breen cup". "They fell madly in love and my Granddad never came home". "See his family refused to accept my Grandmother'. "My Grandfather didn't go home or talk to any of his family for twenty years".' Finally they contacted him and they didn't know what to do whether to go over or what". 'So they decided to book rooms in a hotel and take all the family over". "My mom came from a family of six so they took out a loan to go". "They went over for two weeks and to everyone's amazement it went well and a tradition emerged every two years we go to Ireland". "I have a Grandaunt living in Nenagh to this day". "She's raising her daughter's three children". "I have never met the smallest I'm due to go over this year so I can't wait to see her baby Hanna".

"Ah jaysus", said Claire spitting out her drink.

"What's wrong asked the driver is it too sweet".

"No, no", said Claire. "This Grandaunt of yours it wouldn't be Perpetual O'Brien by any chance would it?"

"Oh my goodness", said the driver, "it is, it is". "Do you know her?"

"Yeah", said Claire, "we know her".

"I'll tell her I met ye I'm going to ring her Sunday".

Claire and Dave sat in shocked silence in the back seat for the remaining ten minutes of the journey. They pulled up outside the hotel and a man stepped forward and opened the door of the escalade for them. Their driver turned around and shook their hands.

"It was lovely to meet some people from home, especially ones who know my own, have a great holiday".

"Thanks", they said as the got out of the escalade.

"Luggage?' Asked the door man.

"No, no", said Dave, "we travel light".

"Delighted to hear that", replied the doorman.

They walked in to the lobby and were blown away by the luxurious red carpet and cheerful décor. They walked over to the desk and checked in.

"Passports please", asked the man behind the desk. "We will keep them safe here for you both you can get them back in the morning".

"But we have already paid", said Dave.

"Oh yes I see that", said the receptionist, "but it is policy".

"That's ok", said Claire.

"We are very tired", said Dave, can we get our key and go to our room.

The receptionist handed them their key card and they got the elevator and went to their room. They were both exhausted and to tired to take in the splendor of their surroundings. They fell into bed in their clothes and when they woke the sun was shining in through a crack in their curtains.

"Wow", said Dave look at this place LCD TV, internet a sitting room in our bedroom. Claire rubbed the painted canvas hanging on the wall.

"It's not a print", she said, "it's a real painting feel it".

Dave walked over and rubbed it. "Wow it's amazing", I whish we could just live here for ever.

"Me too", said Claire.

"Will we ring room service for breakfast?" Dave asked.

"Yeah", said Claire.

"What will we get?" Dave asked.

"Just tell them to surprise us", Claire replied.

They were brought up a breakfast of the juiciest fruit cereal bacon and toasted bagels. "That's the nicest breakfast ever, said Claire, "and imagine it's included in our bill". "This is all mind blowing", said Dave, "thank you so much babe".

"What are you on about", said Claire, "sure aren't you going to be looking after us from here on in? "There is nothing to thank me for".

After they had their breakfast they headed downstairs and outside into the open air. The doorman hailed them a taxi and they asked the driver to take them to Macy's as it was the only department store in New York they could think of. They bought two casual but smart outfits each and two going out outfits each. They returned to the hotel this done and spent the rest of the day basking in the luxury of their surroundings they even ate their dinner in the hotel restaurant, and spent the rest of the evening until they were ready to fall into bed enjoying cocktails at the hotel bar.

"Well", said Dave, "today is the day babe we are going to have to start looking for an apartment and jobs".

"I know", said Claire, "and thanks to our driver they will know soon at home if not already where we are".

"Does that worry you?" Dave asked.

"No", said Claire, "but I think it's hilarious to come all this way to meet the next door neighbors grand nephew".

"It's a small world", said Dave. "I'm glad to be honest let them know we are not going to be sitting around for them to be looking down on us".

"Well", said Claire, 'after what we did to Matthew a bit of a back lash had to be expected like he wouldn't hurt a fly".

"Fuck back to Matthew so", said Dave.

"What", asked Claire?

"Well I'm just thinking if you were having such a good time with Matthew why didn't you stay with him".

"I'll tell you why, said Claire, because he bored me to death smothered me and wasn't half the man you are I love you babe that's why". "The point I was making is a sap like him always gets the sympathy".

"So what will we do go to an estate agents, get a paper?'

"How do you mean?" Claire asked.

"To find somewhere to live?" Dave said.

"Oh I was thinking why don't we take a walk around and see if there are any apartments to let signs in windows'. "We are going to be illegal immigrants Dave we don't want to be going around advertising ourselves'.

"Your right", Claire.

"What areas will we go to?"

"I was thinking Queens, the Bronx said Claire, but where I'd really love to live would be Manhattan".

They got dressed had breakfast and headed out their first day walking around New York. They got a bus down to Queens and there it was facing a park two stories up an apartment to let sign with a mobile number to ring. They took down the number and rang it from the pay phone across the street. We are going to have to look into getting new mobiles because mobiles we cant top up are no good to us over here, said Dave. I know, said Claire but for now we are fine. They rang the number a man answered.

He sounded a pleasant man. "Where are you?" "I'm asking because I am just around the corner from the apartment". "I own the all American diner I'm in here holding interviews". "My 11.30 hasn't shown I can take you up to the apartment now if it suits".

Claire stood huddled beside Dave at the phone box listening intently. She nudged Dave and nodded eagerly.

"Tell him that would be great I've a good feeling about this".

"Did you hear that?" Dave asked. "We are at the phone box across from the apartment". "Right", the man said, "I'll be with you in five minutes". "The caretaker Reese will have the key I left it with him should someone come to view and I was not around". Two minutes later a small baldly pleasantly plump man walked towards them smiling. He looked just how they expected; they just knew it was him.

"Hi Irish", he said, "I seem to be attracting all the illegal immigrants", 'I'm Jamine". "How did you hear about the apartment?"

"We're not illegal", said Dave.

"Sure, sure that's your own business come with me and I'll show ye around". They walked up the stairs the hall way of the building was painted lime green and white and it looked so clean and bright. Jamine knocked on the first apartment on the ground floor. "Reese can I have the key to 2B I've got your new neighbors here".

Reese poked his head out the door to look.

"Oh more Irish, is there any Irish at home in Ireland at this stage", Reese asked.

He handed the key to Jamine.

"And Reese", Jamine turned around, "you're a keeping the building lovely anything broken or anything I should know about".

"No everything is fine".

"I'd be lost without you", said Jamine.

"I'm afraid the apartment has just been painted so it might still smell of paint a bit". "That's fine", said Claire.

They walked in and the sheer size of the apartment made them gasp. And the freshly painted white walls gave the place a lovely fresh clean feel. The door opened into a large living area with the kitchen to the left of it. There were four large windows along the exterior wall. There were two bedrooms and bathroom with shower and bath.

"Is it very expensive?" Claire asked.

"Its $400 a month and a months deposit with two months up front". "But it comes unfurnished". "The last tenants we had in wrecked the place most of the furniture was broken when they left and what wasn't broken wasn't fit to be used".

"That's not a problem", said Claire, "I'd like to have my own furniture anyways especially the bed". "I wouldn't like to sleep on a mattress some stranger had before me".

"So, said Dave, he gently touched the bum bag strapped safely to his waist and hidden under his clothes, do you want to show it to other people make up your mind and get back to us or can we pay you now".

"It's all yours if you can pay me now".

Claire pulled out her purse. "Shit she said", sorry I've got to change my money to dollars".

"That's not a worry", said Jamine, "there is a bank around the corner to your left". Claire said, "will you wait while I run up there?".

"Sure no problem", said Jamine.

Claire went to the bank up to the exchange desk and changed all the money in her purse to dollars except for one 50 euro note that she folded up and put in the little pocked in her wallet with the folded up picture of herself and Matthew and the business card that she had that Matthew had printed up in one of those machines you find in the shopping centers. The card read.

Experienced builder available. Call Matthew and his mobile number beneath.

Claire smiled; her purse would no longer close. I'll give Jamine $5,200 altogether that will be us sorted for a year and give us a great start. She returned to the building and Jamine and Dave were sitting on the steps outside talking she could hear them laughing. "Jamine", said Claire, "could I give you $5,200 altogether and we will be sorted for the year".

"I don't know", said Jamine, "any complaints from the neighbors and your out and I won't be giving you any of that back".

"There won't be any complaints", said Dave.

"I have a good feeling about this", said Jamine, "go on ahead I'll take it". "Now any problems go to Reese he's been taking care of the building for me for the last five years, there's no need to contact me". "The laundry is in the basement no late night parties this is a family building". "Any questions"?

"None", said Claire, "oh one can we paint the apartment any color we like".

"Knock yourselves out".

Claire opened her purse Jamines mouth fell open at the amount of cash she was carrying around with her.

"He caught her by the arms put that away don't be opening your wallet in the street". They went inside the building and back up stairs to the apartment.

"Now, said Jamine you shouldn't be walking around with all that money on you". "And you definatly shouldn't be opening your wallet on the street".

Claire counted out $5,200 and handed it over.

"That's why I want to give you the money to get rid of some of it just incase".

"You know you can open a bank account over here even if you're illegal once you have identification they won't be checking you out".

"Thanks for that", said Dave, he had been wondering what he would do with his stash. Jamine checked the money again "thanks guys welcome to your new home I hope you will be very happy here".

"Thanks", said Dave.

"One minute", said Claire, "did you say you were looking for staff for your diner?"

"You don't want a waitress by any chance do you?"

"Yeah", said Jamine.

"I guess you would be looking cash in hand?"

"Well yeah", said Claire.

"Come on down tomorrow and I'll see what we can do for you".

"Thanks", said Claire, "but I wouldn't be able to start for a fortnight want to get us settled in first".

"That's fine", said Jamine, "come down to me when your ready and I'll see if I am still looking for someone".

Dave and Claire spent the rest of the day looking at furniture and rugs.

"We'll wait until we paint the place before we make up our minds as to what kind of furniture to get", said Dave.

"Your right", said Claire, "I'm tired will we go back to the hotel".

They hailed a taxi on the street and returned to the Gramercy hotel. They went up to their room showered and changed. Claire wondered why Dave always got dressed in the bathroom. Dave wondered if Claire had spotted his money pouch. Showered and changed Claire and Dave went down stairs to the reception.

"Are there any nice restaurants in the area you'd recommend", Claire asked the receptionist?

"What kind of food were you looking for?"

" I'd like Chinese", said Dave.

"Yeah", said Claire, "that sounds good to me".

"There is a lovely Chinese two blocks away our door man will hail you a cab outside". "Thanks", said Claire.

They went outside and got into the taxi and Claire slipped some money out of her purse in the back seat and into her hand she was all paranoid about carrying around that cash since Jamine had warned her. The sooner we open bank accounts the better she whispered to Dave. They got out paid the driver and went into the restaurant to eat. Over dinner they planned out the next day.

"We'll go get paint for the bedrooms", said Claire, "what do you think I'm happy with the living room being white".

"Yeah", said Dave, "but will we paint the bathroom too?"

"Yeah", said Claire, "and that will be enough and when we have that all done we can go get furniture and a television and all that".

They go back to the hotel at one am. The following morning they got up at six am.

"It must be the excitement of it all", said Dave.

"Yeah", said Claire, "I feel like a little child this is the biggest adventure I've ever been on".

8

Matthew got up early showered and changed and cooked himself a fry. He was going down to Travels to see Justine to thank her for calling up the night. Oh how embarrassing he thought me snoring me head off in the chair. Just as he was putting his fry on the plate from the pan he heard the click of the letterbox as letters hit the floor. Matthew took his plate to the table and went out into the hall and picked up the two envelopes than lay on the floor. One was thick and bulky he saw the markings and knew it was from the bank. He walked back into the kitchen sat down and opened his letters as he ate the fry. He left the bank letter until last. The first letter which had seemed harmless to him caused him to seethe with anger it was from the credit union.

Dear Mr. Ryan,

We are writing to you in connection with Mr. Danaher's recent loan request. In your role as guarantor we would request that you contact us at your most recent convience to complete forms that will allow us pay forward the said sum of monies to Mr. Danaher.

Matthew did not bother to finish reading the letter. He left his breakfast and picked up the phone and rang the number on top of the letter.

"Hello how can I help you?" said the voice at the other end?

"Hi" my name is Matthew Ryan a Dave Danaher applied for a loan and put me down as guarantor without my knowledge". "I don't want to be rude but I wouldn't give that fecker the steam off my piss". "Excuse me now but I'm so angry, the cheek of him". "Your grand Matthew", said the voice at the other end of the phone, "I will attach a note to that loan application stating that you are not willing to be guarantor".

"Your fucking right I'm not the stupid fucker the cheek of him".

"Don't worry Mr. Ryan I understand there is no need to worry money can't be paid out without you knowledge". "Your name will be deleted from the application with a note attached explaining why".

"Thank you", said Matthew, "I'm sorry for getting irate".

"You're ok", Mr. Ryan I hope our conversation re assured you, and you will not be in anyway financially liable for this loan".

"Thank you said Matthew, thank you".

Matthew returned to the table picked up a slice of toast and spread marmalade on it. He picked up the other letter. He opened it and was surprised when his bank cards fell from it. I'm just going to view this as the cynical move it is he thought. I wonder what the hell she thinks she is playing at. He washed the dishes and headed down to the travel agents on the way he passed Perpetual walking the boys to school. Matthew pulled up beside them.

"Mrs. O'Brien can I offer you a lift?"

"Ah your grand", said Mrs. O'Brien, "I'd only have to take Hanna out of the pram fold it up by the time we would be in the car they would be late for school".

"Sure I'll pop them in the car if you like", Matthew said looking at the boys, save your legs and go up home".

" I will so", said Perpetual, "if you're sure".

Jesus thought Matthew she looks pale as he drove away from the school after dropping the boys. Matthew called into Travels. Justine called Melanie Matthew is here.

"I guess it's her you want?" Melanie asked.

"Yeah it is", said Matthew.

Justine walked out, "oh Matthew how are you?"

"I'm fine", said Matthew, "I just called in to thank you for calling up the other night". "I'm sorry for giving you a shock and I'm sorry I was asleep".

"Your grand", said Justine.

"I was wondering would you have time for a coffee or are you busy?"

"No", said Justine "I'm free at the moment".

"Do you need me here Melanie?"

"No not at all you go enjoy your coffee".

"Thanks, said Justine".

She had an appointment with Oliver in the bank today but she wasn't worried about it business had picked up immensely. They went down to cakes and things for coffee. "Matthew", Justine said I'm inundated with customers enquiring after you. "You really struck a cord that day on Ormond radio". "They loved you".

Matthew laughed. Catriona was at the counter getting a coffee to take away. She turned around and saw Matthew. She walked up to him and Justine.

"Matthew I'm so sorry for what happened to you".

"Thanks Catriona", but sure I suppose it could have been worse there is nobody dead. "That's a good attitude to have", said Catriona, "I heard you on Ormond radio you sounded so heard broken".

"Ah well", said Matthew, "I still am but what choice do any of us have but to carry on". "I guess your right", said Catriona, "and Justine how are the two of you I mean you, and Yvonne?"

"We're good thanks".

"Yvonne was up there ah its a few months back we gave her some money for advertising on the front of this broucher thing for the fashion show".

" Oh I nearly forgot Matthew", Yvonne said if I saw you to ask you if you were still ok to be in the show", said Justine.

"Tell her I am sure it will pass the time and it's for a good cause".

"Bye now", said Catriona, "I've got to go back up to the office we are very busy". "We were kind of glad Claire wasn't coming back to work Matthew after what she did it would have been hard to work with her". "Your best friend it's terrible".

"I didn't know she wasn't going back to work", said Matthew, "why is that?"

"She is in America according to her call, staying there for good I presume Dave is with her". "I thought you would know".

"No", said Matthew, it turns out that there are an infinite number of things I don't know by the looks of things".

"I've got to go if there is anything I can do just let me know", said Catriona as she walked out of the shop.

Mrs. O'Brien did not go straight up home instead she went straight up to Shelia's. "Shawn rang from America there last night".

"Oh", said Shelia, that's nice I'll put the kettle on. "Is he coming over?"

"Yeah the end of August but that's not why I'm telling you". "You know the way he works for a limousine company". "Well you'll never guess who he drove from JFK airport to a hotel Friday evening Claire and Dave I don't know whether to tell Matthew or not". "What do you think I should do?"

"Oh", said Shelia, I say you may as well tell him sure he might be glad to know they are out of the country and he won't have to be seeing them again".

"Your right I'll tell him, the minute I see the car in the drive I'll go out to him".

"Are you ok?" Justine asked Matthew.

"Yeah I'm fine I'm not too surprised actually I had a loan I applied for with the bank it was put in my account Claire cleaned me out 250,000 euro the loan was for and she took 200,000". "I'm sure she was getting a lot of pressure from Dave to do it but still and all I'd say they were afraid they could be prosecuted or something I'd say that had a lot to do with them going"." At least they had the common decency not to be sticking around here after all they did".

"I suppose so", said Justine, "but can you do nothing about it go to the guards or anything".

"No I had Claire's name put on the account so she was entitled to take money out". "The solicitor told me that what they did whilst morally wrong was not legally wrong". "The devils own have the devils luck", said Justine.

"That's not the best of it after cleaning out the account Claire had the bald faced cheek to ring up threatening me looking for her clothes".

Matthew and Justine burst out laughing.

"They aren't living in the real world at all are they?"

"No", said Matthew. "I can't believe what I saw in either of them they turn my stomach now". "I couldn't stand the sight of them I'm glad they are gone and I hope they never come back".

"What if it's only a holiday", said Justine.

"Let's pray its not", said Matthew.

"Thanks for getting Yvonne that babysitting job". "She seems to spend all of her time with Mrs. O'Brien and those kids these days".

"So when will I have to rehearse for this show?"

"I'll ask her and get back to you".

"This was nice", said Matthew; "we should do it more often".

"I still owe you dinner", said Justine.

"I'll hold you to that", said Matthew.

Justine went back to the travel agents and Matthew went up home. Perpetual saw the car pulling into the drive I'll give him five minutes, she said and then I'll head into him. She picked up Hanna and put her into the pram so she wouldn't be pulling anything while they were out in Matthews she was beginning to crawl a bit lately and she could pull something on top of herself in the blink of an eye. She walked up to the door and knocked. Matthew opened the door the tears streaming down his face.

"She's gone to America Mrs. O'Brien I'll never see her again".

Perpetual stepped in front of the pram and gave Matthew a hug.

"That's what I was coming to tell you Shawn my grand nephew do you remember him he drove them from JFK airport". "I'm so sorry Matthew".

"She cleaned me out", Mrs. O'Brien, "so she did I'm destroyed".

"How do you mean?"

"Well I re-mortgaged the house to invest in a housing development with the way the economy is it fell through but I forgot to cancel the loan and they emptied my account the loan was for 250,000 they took 200.000". "I'll be paying back that money for thirty years and they will be spending it for a few weeks".

"Your well rid Matthew they are bad ones make no mistake". "But what goes around comes around Matthew they will get theirs in due course".

"I know that", said Matthew, "but how is it I miss her so much". "How can I be missing someone who would do the likes of this?"

"That's love for you Matthew that's just the way it is".

Matthews mobile phone rang he wiped his face walked over to the mantle piece picked up his phone and answered it.

"Hello".

"Hello" is this Matthew Ryan?

"Yes".

"This is Leanne from Ormond radio". "I'm ringing on behalf of Patricia she was wondering if you would come back on the show Saturday week". "Loads of people are texting ringing e-mailing asking what happened to you afterwards how you are coping". "Oh really", said Matthew, "sure why not I'm doing nothing else".

"Thanks so", Matthew, "will you come in to the studio to us?"

"Yeah I will why not".

"Right so", said Leanne, "9am Saturday week".

"Thanks Matthew" see you then.

"No bother Leanne talk to you".

Matthew turned to Perpetual when he hung up. "That was Ormond radio they want me back again".

"That's great", said Mrs. O'Brien, "what will you talk about?"

"God I don't know rightly", said Matthew, "but I'm sure it will be ok they will ask me questions and I will answer them".

Claire and Dave spent two days painting their new home. They painted the bedroom navy and red. Dave had picked the colors Claire thought it would be terrible but she was surprised how nice it looked. They were heading into their fifth day in New York the time was flying.

"We will go shopping for furniture television and all that tomorrow", said Dave I want to have a weeks relaxation before we start the tiring routine of work". "I want to do some sight seeing".

"That's a good idea", said Claire. "Do you think we should get some kind of security system on the apartment this is New York after all".

"We will ask Reese tomorrow", said Dave.

They returned to the hotel tired but happy, had lunch and retired to bed. They were woken the following morning by the bedside phone ringing. There is a large number of boxes in reception for you they are on the way up to your room on the luggage cart. Claire answered the phone half asleep.

"Thanks so", she said and put the phone down.

"Who was that?" Dave asked.

"Some boxes on their way up to us".

Dave laughed," you still asleep that's our clothes stupid".

Dave rang down to reception "hello this is Dave Danaher room 307 you just rang to tell us some boxes are on the way". "Have they already left reception or are they still down there?"

"They are being loaded on the luggage cart as we speak".

"Oh can you keep them down there they are clothes gifts for friends here and we will only have to carry them all back down to drop them over to them".

"That explains it said the man in reception we thought you were moving in here permanently".

Dave laughed, "so can you hang on to them there?"

"Yeah no problem but you must come immediately and remove them".

"Not a problem", said Dave, "we will be there in ten minutes".

Claire groaned, "don't tell me we have to get up please don't tell me that".

"I'm afraid so", said Dave.

"They quickly brushed their teeth threw on clothes and went down stairs to reception". "You won't get all that into a taxi", the man in reception said. "Would you like to have our hotel limousine service take you to where ever it is you are going?"

"That would be great", said Claire.

The man at reception made a call he turned around and said to Dave and Claire." Please wait outside and there will be someone to collect you directly".

"Thanks", they said, "and Dave went to push the trolley with their clothes in boxes out the door".

"Please do wait", said the man at reception, "your things will be brought out front". Dave and Claire went outside and their trolley was pushed out behind them. A black escalade pulled up and Shawn jumped out.

"Hello folks you have a delivery to make I believe".

"Yeah", said Claire, as their clothes were being loaded in to the back of the van.

"Well", said Shawn "jump in."

They jumped into the back. Shawn jumped into the driver's seat and pressed a button and the partition between them and him rolled down.

"So where to folks?" He asked.

Claire gave him the address in Queens.

"So you are here to stay", said Shawn.

"No, no", said Dave, "we are simply dropping these boxes over to a friend they are gifts we brought with us".

"I was talking to aunty Perpetual and I know all about you". "Back in Ireland they are saying leaving is the only shred of common decency you both have shown in all of this no one wants to be looking at your ugly faces". "I was like wow; said Shawn, like you must have really upset a lot of people".

Claire looked at Dave, she expected him to say something in their defense he kept looking out the window of the escalade avoiding her stare.

"Well, said Claire fine I left my husband and not in the way I would have liked to but how can you leave someone and not hurt them?"

"And yeah your aunty and I never were close and do you know why they all backing Matthew up it's because he is a pathetic useless lump the kind that always needs validation and reassurance and all the women want to mother him". "That's why".

"Did he not take care of you baby", Shawn asked.

"That's all I've got to say", Claire said it's none of your business anyways.

"Point taken", said Shawn.

They arrived at the address in Queens. Shawn pulled up outside.

"How much is that?", asked Claire.

"$60 Dollars sweetie".

"That's highway robbery", said Dave, "it only took you fifteen minutes".

"I don't set the rates", said Shawn, "you'll have to take it up with my boss". "So, said Shawn are you going to pay or have we a problem".

All color drained from Dave's face. "I was only buzzing of you mate". "Having a laugh, a bit of craic that's all"." No there is no problem here".

"And", said Claire, "if there was a problem you would know all about it believe me". "See those bruises they are well faded now on my babies face know how he got them". "Two thugs came into my Dave's bookies shop back home trying to start a protection racket and he took on both of them ran them from the shop". "And they will never come back because they know what they will get if they do".

"Is that so", said Shawn. "I'm seeing you in a whole new light man", he said to Dave. "You seemed like a total light weight to me but a regular little gangster then are you?" "Well I don't like to brag", said Dave.

"So", said Shawn the last of the boxes sitting on the path outside. "Do you want me to help ye take those boxes from the side walk to your new apartment".

Claire and Dave looked at each other.

"Jesus" said Claire, how often do we have to tell everyone it's not our apartment. Shawn cut across her. "Do your thing babes it isn't nothing to do with me". "Its ok honey", said Dave, "I think we can trust him".

"Yeah sure help us but we are not paying you", said Claire.

"Yes maim", said Shawn to Claire.

It only took them twenty minutes to take the stuff up.

"This is a nice neighborhood Shawn told them".

"Do you think we need to get some kind of security system on the apartment", Claire asked.

"It never hurts", Shawn said, "but New York isn't all as bad as people seem to think". "I know the man who owns this building a great man Jamine have you met him?"

"Yeah", said Claire.

"Jesus", said Dave "is there anyone you don't know?"

"About security", Claire cut in?

"You know it isn't where you live it's how you live", said Shawn.

"I hear you", said Claire.

"I'm going to buy cigarettes", said Dave ,"does anyone want anything from the shop?" "No", said Shawn "thanks". "Actually babe will you get some biscuits and tea bags and milk you'll have a cup wont you Shawn?"

"I will so thanks".

Dave walked out the door and Shawn left a few minutes to be sure he was gone.

"Claire babe?"

"Yeah what", Claire replied.

"I hope you know what your doing you seem a nice girl but that Dave I just hope you know what you've got yourself into".

They heard someone walking up the stairs and then the door opened Dave was back from the shop. The three of them sat on the floor talking.

"So", said Shawn, tell me about your self Dave were you the local robin hood or more the local scar face?"

"I don't understand what you're asking me", said Dave.

'Well", said Shawn running off people who run money rackets that's no mean feat".

"Oh I see", said Dave laughing, "no I'm a whole new breed of gangster".

"Dave's got connections all over the world haven't you Dave", said Claire.

Shawn had to develop a sudden episode of coughing to disguise his laugh. He thought he would piss himself.

"So Dave do you know what you should do over here you should start a hip hop club". "Even have a little studio down stairs where you could write about your experiences and all that".

Dave smiled to himself. "That wouldn't be a bad idea at all".

Sean stood, "well it's been interesting I'm going to head back incase they are looking for me".

Claire walked Shawn downstairs, "thanks for all your help Shawn".

"Your welcome Claire mind yourself do you hear".

"Of course I will", Claire replied.

Shawn drove back to the hotel and Dave and Claire spent the day unpacking their clothes and hanging them in their new wardrobes and admiring the view from their windows.

"We are going to be so happy here" Dave said to Claire as they sat on the floor in each others arms looking at the bright lights that shone all round them.

"I can feel that too babe", said Claire.

They returned to the hotel and went straight to sleep. The following morning they got up ate breakfast and headed straight out to buy furniture. There was such variety in New York it was unreal. The concrete jungle built on dreams. Claire felt so alive here as though a great freedom had swept over her. The emptiness inside here was gone. They went from store to store in the morning buying nothing walking around in a daze. At one o'clock they went for lunch.

"Right", said Claire, "lets just decide to get the essentials for now we need a table and chairs a bed and a suite of furniture". "A television and linen for the bed a hover a set of saucepans a kettle a toaster a microwave oh yeah and can opener".

"Right so", said Dave "how do you want to do this?

"Right", said Claire, "the main thing is that the stuff is delivered early Monday morning or before then that will give us two days to relax in the hotel doing nothing maybe take in a few sights".

"How's about this we make a list I'll get the bed suite of furniture and all that you get the linen hover and all that, said Dave".

"Deal", said Claire, "but be careful of the prices we don't want to be broke she handed Dave a big wad of money under the table in the restaurant".

"How much is in that", Dave asked.

"$10,000" Claire replied, "but that doesn't mean you got to spend it all".

"Of course", said Dave.

Claire ran around Macey's picking up all the items on her list for under $600. Dave found a small furniture shop on the corner he fell in love with a sofa he saw with deep cushions and a recliner chair.

"How much is that", Dave asked the lady in the shop?

"Its $7,000" she replied.

"And the recliner chair?" Dave asked.

"$1,500 each".

"I'll get that sofa and two chairs", said Dave.

"He handed over the money how soon can you deliver?"

"We are a small but exclusive store we will deliver immediately".

"That's great", said Dave.

"If you'll just give us the address, the lady said".

Dave gave her the address in queens and ran to Maceys where he knew Claire was shopping. He ran straight to the household section. She was there looking at kettles. "Which do you think honey", she asked seeing Dave approaching.

"I don't mind whatever you decide".

"Can you give me they key and money for a taxi they are delivering the furniture as we speak and I want to be there before them or they won't be able to get in"

Claire handed Dave $300 "you're a great shopper I can't wait to see our new furniture". "I'll get the stuff from my list and meet you back there in two hours".

"That's great babe", said Dave, he turned around with the keys and wad of money in his hand ran outside waited ten minutes before a taxi stopped and when he arrived at the apartment the furniture delivery van was just pulling up outside. He paid the driver and ran over to them. There were three men inside the four of them took an hour to get the furniture up stairs to the apartment. Dave handed them $200 when they had finished and put the remaining $50 into his pocket. An hour later Claire arrived laden down with bags. Dave could see her getting off the bus at the stop across the street. He ran to meet her and help her carry the bags up.

"I'm sorry I was so long Dave it took me for ever to decide on what stuff to get". "Is all our furniture up there already?"

"It sure is", said Dave.

"Ha, ha", said Claire, "you are talking like an American already".

They both laughed.

Claire walked in the door of the apartment. "Oh Dave the living room furniture is lovely". "I can't wait to see the bed".

Claire turned and walked into what they had decided would be their room.

"Dave where is the bed for fucks sake your not telling me that this is all you got with $10,000".

"I told you to be careful of the prices". "We have to keep some aside incase something goes wrong". "You never listen of course why would you care".

"What did you say?" said Dave he ran towards Claire.

It was 6am Claire woke up curled in the corner in the room.

"Hey babe you awake", asked Dave.

Claire nodded.

"Now I'm going to go to Mac Donald's get us some breakfast". "You go wash yourself I'm going to look after you why did you have to go upsetting me last night you know how hard

I am trying to make things nice for you". "Why can't you be nice?" "Good girl go wash and I'll have breakfast for you".

Claire went to the living room and took towels from the upturned bag. She took in shower gel toilet paper and shampoo and conditioner. After her shower she stood in front of the mirror to dry herself and cried. She heard Dave come back in the door she went to the room wrapped in her bath sheet and put on jeans and a hoodie.

"Here you go honey", said Dave.

"Thanks", said Claire.

"How's about we go shopping for the rest of the stuff we need after this". "We could even check out of the hotel early".

" I don't mind", said Claire.

"Jesus, said Dave don't sound too excited anyways I'm trying so hard here".

"No, no Dave said Claire; I'd love to finish the shopping". "Hopefully they will deliver today".

"Well", said Dave, "if we go to the store I went to yesterday they will deliver today". "They are open seven days a week ten to ten so we will have loads of time to pick things out".

"Ok", said Claire.

They left the building and walked over to the bus stop. Dave took Claire's hand in his and squeeze it Claire squeezed his hand back. The bus came they got on it and went down town back to the shop where Dave had gone shopping the day before.

"Oh sir", your back, said the lady as she walked towards them.

"We need a table and chairs and two double beds today", said Matthew.

"Come with me".

They followed her through the shop.

"Dave", said Claire, "I'm no trying to annoy you but do you think it might be very expensive here".

Dave laughed he turned to the lady, "Claire's the sensible one in this relationship". "Don't worry about it babe I'm willing to blow any amount on you, your worth it."

"Ah said the lady isn't that nice to hear". Claire nodded she opened her bag and searched frantically through it. There was her wallet she opened it there was no more than $5,000 left in it. Dave must have taken it out last night.

"Everything ok babe?" Dave asked.

"Yeah", said Claire its fine.

Dave picked out a double bed with memory foam mattress, "how much is that? $5,000". "Claire babe feel it its great sit on it".

Claire sat on the bed she then got up and pressed her hand down on the mattress and watched as her hand print disappeared.

"So what's the verdict?" Dave asked.

"Its great said Claire and the bed I love all the carved designs". "We will take two of them and the two blanket boxes that go with them and four lockers". Claire laughed. Can you think of anything else we might need honey? Dave asked.

"Bed side lamps", Claire replied.

If he had taken her money she was going to see as much as possible of it got spent, he wasn't going to go piss it up against a wall if she could help it.

"You might like these ones we have in stock; they are Irish crystal designed by Louise Kennedy, a little something from home so you don't feel home sick".

"How do you know we are Irish?" Claire asked.

"Well with that accent, the girl replied you are hardly Mexican".

"Oh my god", said Claire those lamps are lovely we'll take four.

"And now", said Dave we need a table and chairs.

"Oh," said Claire, "I love this one".

"That's a lovely piece", said the lady. "Hand crafted a one of a kind black marble and Mexican pine".

"How much?" Dave asked.

"$2,500", said the lady.

"How's about this babe you get to choose the table and chairs I won't interfere and I choose the television?"

"Ok", said Claire, "I want this one".

"Ok so", said the lady, "and do you want them delivered today?".

"Yes", said Dave.

"Have we time to shop for a television?"

"There is a Sony centre across the road I'm sure by the time everything is loaded and ready to go you will be on your way home".

Claire and Dave left the shop hand in hand and headed into the Sony centre.

"What is your top of the range television", Dave asked the first sales assistant to come there way.

He showed them to a television high definition with home cinema system built in DVD player 50 inch flat screen with stand.

"That might be a bit big for our apartment", said Claire.

"I thought I was picking this?" Dave said.

"You are said Claire don't mind me fire away".

"I'll take it", said Dave, "when can you deliver?"

"First thing in the morning", said the sales assistant. "Are you not going to ask the price?" The sales assistant asked?

"How much is it", asked Dave?

" $8,000".

Dave opened his wallet and counted out $8,000.

"You shouldn't be walking around with so much money on you sir", said the sales assistant, "are you new to New York?"

"Yeah", said Claire, "we are almost here two weeks now".

"Oh, how are you liking it?"

"So far we love it", said Dave.

Claire and Dave went out got a taxi and went back to the apartment they were home an hour before the delivery truck arrived.

"Hey babe" said Dave, "you sit down put your feet up". "Once the furniture arrives I'll go over to the hotel check us out". "Have we much stuff in the room?"

"Just our clothes", said Claire.

"I'll run up grab the stuff and get us a Chinese on the way back". "How does that sound?"

"It sounds lovely", said Claire.

Dave walked over and started the gas fire in the apartment.

"Now babe you'll be lovely and comfortable".

The buzzer went that's our furniture babe don't you move I'll look after this. They brought up the beds table and chairs and lockers and blanket boxes. They put the beds together in the rooms and the mattresses on top of them for them. Dave gave them $100 each as a tip. When they had gone Dave turned to Claire.

"I'll run over to the hotel now", get us sorted.

"Ok so Dave", said Claire, "Don't forget they have our passports".

"Grand I'll get them you just relax babe you won't feel it and I will be home with the dinner".

When Dave had left Claire took the Macys bag with the bed linen to the room and dressed the bed. She loved the cotton sheets they were so soft, and the duvet set the room looked lovely she couldn't wait to get into the bed that night. Claire put the kettle and toaster on the counter top, and the hover in the press under the sink. Claire went back out to the sofa sat down and fell asleep. Dave came home with a huge bag of Chinese food and the remainder of their stuff from the hotel.

"Do you know what I just remembered I never bought any cutlery", said Claire.

"Don't worry about it", said Dave,

"I got plastic ones from the take away and we can make a list of what we still need tomorrow and go get it along with some grocery shopping".

"Yeah, said Claire".

Claire fell asleep again straight after eating. Dave carried her down to bed took off her shoes and socks and covered her up. He went up to the kitchen tidied the rubbish away and joined Claire in bed and soon they were both asleep. The following morning Dave gave Claire breakfast in bed. After breakfast Claire decided to run down to the All American diner to see if there was a job going. Dave decided to stay in and organize cable television for them. Jamine sat with the paper in one of the fifties style booths. There was a juke box on each table and it reminded Claire of Eddie Rockets in limerick where her and Matthew used go for lunch after they went shopping. She was surprised how much she had been thinking of Matthew these days she had thought she would never be rid of him. She often thought of phoning him but she wouldn't know what to say.

"Hello there", said Jamine how are the Irish settling in?

"We are good Jamine thanks". "It's lovely up there and the gas fire makes it really homely".

"So what can I do for you, you're not down here looking for a job are you?"

"I am indeed", said Claire.

"You couldn't have gone through that big wad of money already have you?"

Claire looked at the floor for a split second just long enough not to cry and then she said with a smile.

So is there a job going?

"Sure is I need someone for the breakfasts and lunch". "6am to 4pm". "The breakfast crew aren't big tippers it picks up after that though".

"I'll take it", said Claire.

"Those are lovely nails you got there". "Those hands don't look like they ever did much work you do know you will have to do cleaning here as well". "People will be shouting complaining".

"I'll be fine", said Claire, "I will do whatever I have to I promise".

"Ok you can start tomorrow morning at 6".

"Thanks", said Claire; she went up home and told Dave.

"That's great babe", said Dave, "you starting to act like a real grown up your first ever full time job at 28 years of age". "Let's hope you don't get fired it won't be easy for someone like you with no qualifications or experience to get work".

"But I do have experience I've been a receptionist for a year". "I have qualifications from FAS".

"Ah bless your heart babe", said Dave putting his arm around her, "those aren't real qualifications those are only pretend made up things back home so they can take people off the dole". "I'm only telling you this Claire so you won't embarrass yourself over here telling people you have FAS qualifications they will laugh at you". "Ah Jesus Claire you're not crying again are you".

"No I'm not", said Claire, "I'm just tired and my eyes are running".

"Well go wash your face so and you had better think about getting some shopping in for the week".

Ten minutes later Claire came out of the bathroom.

"Do you want to come with me to the shop Dave?"

"No", said Dave.

"I'll need moncy".

"Didn't I leave $5,000 in your wallet you should be able to feed us and pay the bills with that for a long time".

"Yeah, yeah I suppose I will", said Claire.

"I'm going down town to buy a lap top with wireless internet", said Dave.

"I might open an on line betting shop or something". "I need to keep an eye on my emails too".

"I saw an internet café just down the street".

"Don't be daft", Dave laughed, "go get the shopping I'm hungry".

9

The phone rang.

"Hello", said Matthew.

"Good morning Matthew its Yvonne mam said you would still do the fashion show can you believe its three months since the day I asked you almost".

"Three weeks to go Yvonne, said Matthew that's practically a month".

"Yeah I guess so we are starting rehearsals Monday". "The DJ will be here".

"That's great", said Matthew.

"Matthew", said Yvonne, "under the circumstances I understand if you would prefer not be the groom for the mock wedding".

"That would be good Yvonne I would do what ever else you want".

"Would you do the men's clothes for "Dress Nice and Smartly" everyone else has their own people to model them?"

"Will you call down to the shop and contact them".

"I'll do that today Yvonne".

"Thanks Matthew".

"Oh Yvonne how's your mother?"

"She's grand weren't you out to lunch with her there the other day?"

"Yeah", said Matthew, "I think the three of us might be heading out for dinner after this fashion show". "Would that be ok with you?"

"Yeah whatever", said Yvonne?

" Listen I'll see you Monday and go down and get your clothes sorted".

"I will do, bye Yvonne".

Matthew went down to the shop to get his clothes sorted with "Dress Nice and Smartly". The days were flying and slowly Matthew was surprised to find he was feeling content within himself. The following morning Matthew had his return visit to Ormond radio a little over two months since his first appearance. It was a nice sunny evening. Matthew called into Perpetual on the way to the pub to play cards with the lads.

"I am going on Ormond radio again tomorrow I was wondering if Ciaran and Cian would like to come with me for the drive the studio is big there will be loads of room". "They are all yours Matthew if they want to go". "I'd love a Saturday morning to myself or as good as Hanna is too little to be demanding yet".

"Will I go in and say it to them now so?" Matthew asked.

"Go on ahead", said Perpetual.

The boys were delighted they were going to be on radio.

"I'll collect you at seven so".

"I'll have them ready", said Mrs. O'Brien, "would you look there is Seorsha outside your door you better go don't get too drunk now tonight you don't want a head on you in the morning".

Matthew came home early and was up at six in the morning. He collected two excited little boys from Mrs. O'Brien and headed to Mc Donald's in Roscrea where they had breakfast then back to town and in to Ormond radio. Matthew was so glad of the company. He was a different man this morning going into the studio. Patricia was already there when Matthew came .

"Jesus she said you are really cutting it fine I was starting to worry". "And who are these little men?"

"My neighbor's grand children".

"Oh right have ye come to mind him then?"

Two chairs were put beside the chair Matthew was to sit in.

"Now boys", said Derek the producer, "here is some sweets for you". "I'll show you all around the place after if ye are good and for the life of ye don't touch anything".

"I'm twelve", said Cian, "and I know not to touch things and Ciaran is only five he can't reach nothing".

"That's great", said Derek, "now we have to be very quiet while there is talking in the studio ok".

"Yeah", replied Cian and Ciaran.

Claire sat in the internet café on the street, to delay the time before she went home. She opened and checked her internet account. No one from home had contacted her in a long time. She had got an e-mail from them all at work when she had come over first saying best of luck in your new life Catriona, Tom, Ashley and Adrian but that was it. She had e-mailed them but they had not replied. Claire was home sick she typed Ormond radio into the goggle search bar and went to the counter and asked for headphones. She came back clicked on search and then opened the Ormond radio home page and clicked on the icon that said listen. In five four they were on air. Matthew was barely sitting down he didn't even have the ear phones on.

"Hello", everyone said Patricia, "and this morning we have brought back a special guest for you Matthew you may remember him from our valentines stories show". "Here's a clip from that show now".

Patricia pressed a button and Matthews voice came echoing back to him from what now seemed like a life time ago. Oh my God thought Claire. She longed to hear Matthew's voice it was so strange it was not long ago that it grated her nerves yet here she was longing to hear him say something anything.

Matthew cringed, "oh I sound like such a looser in that clip Patricia".

Patricia laughed then put her finger to her lips they were back on air.

"So Matthew tell me this how are things with you now?"

"Well Patricia it's like this. Can I just say first?"

"Please do", said Patricia.

"I know I will never be getting back with my wife. I was talking a load of nonsense there". "Sure I forgive her but have her back in a heart beat.... no."

"Do you still love her Matthew?"

"Yeah Patricia, I love her enough to hate her"." See I think it's like a death I'm currently going through the stage of anger last time I was on I was in denial who knows if you have me back I may be in acceptance of the whole thing".

Matthew began to laugh.

"At the end of the day you have to put things into perspective and once you have your health it's never to late to start over".

"You sound a lot more cheerful anyway", said Patricia.

"You see I am". "And I've looked at and I appreciate how I helped sabotage our relationship". "I think that I put a lot of pressure in our relationship to". "I never just relaxed I always had to be ringing sending gifts being foolishly extravagant". "I was looking for someone to complete me". "I was love starved and I put pressure on Claire to fill that void". "I wanted the Hollywood marriage with matching clothes and I put a lot of pressure on my self to provide all these things". "I realize now what you should look for is some one you want to share your life with you". "I know I am a unit complete within myself". "I do not need anyone to complete me but I would be more than happy to share my life with someone who would like to share theirs with me".

"That's very deep for this hour of the morning Matthew".

"Yeah", said Matthew, "I believe there is a misconception fed to us throughout our lives that we are incomplete and that we need our significant other to make us a whole".

"I've done a lot of thinking on this one Patricia and I think in order for us to have a relationship that works we must first allow ourselves become the person we want to become achieve our own goals".

" Provide the space for each other within our relationships for each individual to progress and grow". "It is unfair on the other person to invest our happiness in them". "It puts to much pressure on another person to expect them some how to be the answer to all our dreams". "We ourselves must strive to be happy we cannot expect someone else to do that for us". "I'm not saying that that cannot be done in the realms of a relationship I'm just saying that each person must respect the others right to develop themselves and achieve what is important to them". "I think that is how I sabotaged myself". "I put to much pressure on Claire I narrowed my focus to her and her alone; I gave her no space I monopolized her". "I gave her no space".

“Do you really believe that Matthew”, asked Patricia, “she did have an affair with your best friend?”

“Yes Patricia”, I think that there may have been a bit of the whole girls thinking if your not, oh how can I say this nicely I think some girls want a real man you know like Scar Face or James Bond”. “Claire thought I was weak you look at me in disbelief Patricia she did she told me so”. “She said I should have been fighting for her and instead I was a sniveling wreck or words to that effect”.

“Matthew I really think you are being too nice taking blame onto your self”.

“Now that’s the phrase I was looking for Claire thought I was too nice”. “Look Patricia this isn’t the end of my world life goes on”. “Sure I have good days and bad days”. “I do miss her like but looking back I feel that I deserved to be treated better too”.” I have got closer to my friends and neighbors”.” And I’d like to take this opportunity to thank everyone who asked how I was called up”. “To Justine in Travels for the coffee, chats”. “You’re fast becoming my bbf babe”.

“What’s a bbf Matthew?” Patricia asked.

“It’s a best friend forever”.

“Oh and are we becoming bbf’s too”.

“Of course”, said Matthew, “but we’ll have to hang out a bit chill relax you know”.

“Oh they want us to take a quick call”.

“Hello Anna?

“ Hello Patricia”, I want to talk to Matthew.

“I’m here go ahead”, said Matthew.

“My name is Anna and I heard you on the radio both times”. “You see I live with my boyfriend for three years”. “He’s not nice all the time”.

“ I see Anna and tell me this when you say all the time how do you mean is he mean to you once a year, once a week, once a day”.

“Maybe once a day for the past few years, and when he is not, not being nice we are walking on egg shells waiting for him to be not nice”.

Patricia and Matthew looked at each other sadly.

"You say we do you have children?"

"Yeah one he is six". "He's not my boyfriends".

"Do you want to tell us the form the not being nice takes?"

"No Matthew I don't want to talk about it".

"Ok Anna don't worry". "Can I help you in any way?"

"Matthew", said Anna, "I want to know would you have ever left her?" "Like it sounds like she wasn't nice to you either?"

"Anna," said Matthew, "can I ask you one question have you ever in any way been physically assaulted".

There was a long silence on the phone.

"It's ok Anna you don't have to answer this". "Anna I don't think our circumstances can be compared". "Anna each and every person in this world deserves happiness". "You don't need this man who scares you, and you sound scared to me on the phone". "We pass this way but once, and we are here for a good time not a long time".

"Anna please get out of this situation".

"Can you give your number to Derek and we will ring you back off the air".

"I will", said Anna "thanks Matthew". Anna hung up.

Patricia pressed a button and played a song she had queued earlier.

"Jesus Patricia do any of us know how lucky we are", said Matthew while they were off the air.

"No we don't", said Patricia, "I'm so sorry I wasn't expecting that you handled it well". "We're back in 5, 4, 3," said Derek.

"So Matthew what advise have you for our listeners having come out the other side of this whole thing?"

"Well", said Matthew, "you are a whole human being with in your self no lesser or greater than any other don't look for someone to define you, you define you look for an equal partner with whom you would be happy to share your life, not someone who wants to control your life". "And another thing love should not be demanding, or cruel or make you live in fear that's another thing entirely that sure as hell isn't love". Yeah sure you're going to have your ups and downs, but if things deteriorate to a situation where you're in fear whether you are male or female get the hell out". "I'm not saying all day everyday should be a bed of roses or you leave him but Jesus life is to short to waste years in unhappiness until your old bitter and twisted with a wasted life behind you". "And I'm referring to any situation that makes you unhappy more than you are happy, be it home, work, whatever, regardless of the persons relationship to you". Claire clicked the x icon on the top of the screen and closed down the Ormond radio home page. She clicked the x icon again and the computer returned to the main screen. She removed the headphones from her ears and wiped tears from her eyes. She went to the main desk handed back the headphones paid and headed home with a lump in her throat.

"So Matthew tell me this too get back onto a brighter subject", said Patricia, "are you back on the dating scene?"

"Na Patricia it's too soon".

There was a click.

"There listeners Derek has just taken a picture of Matthew it will be up on the Ormond radio website for all to see". "Believe me ladies you wouldn't be disappointed". "So are you happy Matthew?"

"I have good days and bad days to some extent I'm grieving her and to some extent there is a part of me that would love to hear she is miserable". "Is that evil?"

Patricia laughed "na I'd say it's only human".

"Will we take a look at a few of these texts I'm so sorry people Matthew's half hour seems to fly whenever we have him in here with us".

Matthew you look hot Yvonne Nenagh. "And there is a lovely smilie face after that for you Matthew". "Derek have you that picture up already on the web site?" Patricia asked. Derek shook his head through the glass.

"I know Yvonne", said Matthew; "she's Justine who owns travels where I bought my tickets daughter". "She and the transition year students are running a charity fashion show for St. Vincent de Paul the end of May some time and I'm modeling in it".

"It's up now", Derek said.

"Right ladies if you want to see what Matthew looks like check out Ormond radio". "The Saturday morning show". "Well folks I'm afraid that is where we will have to leave it". "One sec", said Matthew, "can the boys say hello to a few people"?.

"Hello Nanny, Shelia, Seorsha, everyone in school everyone who knows us", said Ciaran.

"Do you want to say anything Cian", Patricia asked?

"He's too little", said Ciaran, "he's shy".

The credits played over the last of Ciaran's words.

'So', said Derek will I show you boys around is that ok with you Matthew?

"Yeah its fine", said Matthew.

"So Matthew", said Patricia, "wow I wasn't expecting that girl Anna's phone call, you handled it very well are you really going to ring her back?"

"Of course", said Matthew. "Derek before you go, said Matthew have you a number for that girl?"

"Yeah Matthew on top of the desk" he nodded towards a piece of paper. Matthew went over and picked it up. He took out his mobile and rang.

"Hi Anna its Matthew".

"Hello", came the voice, "I can't talk for long".

"That's ok Anna I'm going to give you my number you can ring it any time". "You know your doctor will have the numbers of people who can help you". "Places you can go". "I'm a builder I'll be there in a minute and change the locks". "You can get a temporary restraining order until you can go to court and have a better arrangement reached". "You can have a better happy stress free life, you know that".

"Thanks Matthew I've got to go get the dinner".

"Listen to me Anna I mean it any time day or night you ring me ok".

"Thanks Matthew".

"You can also go to the citizens advise bureau they will be able to help you give you information".

"Thanks Matthew I really got to go".

"Well", said Patricia, "that's all you can do, she will do what she is going to do".

"I suppose so".

"So Patricia how's the show going for you?"

"It's after taking off very well thank god".

"I'm glad for you", said Matthew, "I think that talking that time really helped me as well". "I was so lost but in a space of under three months things are really starting to pick up". "You would have thought that this would have been the end of my world, but its far from it, in fact I'm starting to think that I'm happier than I ever was". "I'd like to talk to people in a bad place and tell them that things get better". "I'd like to tell them that if they are unhappy for whatever reason move on". "Claire did the right thing if she was unhappy". "I would love to be able to say to people that happiness is the most important thing in the world people should strive to be happy".

"Happy people don't kill people threaten people, rob people".

"The world would be a much better place if we took all our energy and put it into being happy". 'Am I talking shit?"

"No Matthew but you sound like you've been thinking way too much".

They were both laughing and never heard the executive producer open the door of the studio.

"Quick, quick" he shouted there are already two thousand comments on the picture of Matthew on the Ormond radio home page.

"What', said Patricia.

They opened the page on the lap top on the desk.

"Wow", said Patricia. "Matthew they love you imagine how many people must have been listening". "Look read the comments they are all asking you questions about their problems".

"Matthew I want to give you an hour's show every Sunday morning". "I can see it now it will be great".

"But", said Matthew, "I'm not qualified to give advise".

"No", said the Producer, "but you can give your opinion and direct people to the correct place to get someone who is qualified to help". "I know you have no experience of this but we will guide you through the whole process".

"Yes", said Patricia, "if you do it I will come be with you in studio for the first few shows get you started".

"I hate Sundays anyways boring day".

"That's it so first show next Sunday".

The executive producer put out his hand and Matthew shook it.

"Jesus", he said to Patricia when he had gone, "this is so exciting".

"Yeah isn't it we will get loads of time to hang out now".

Patricia nodded towards Derek and Ciaran and Cian as they came down the corridor, "here come the troops". "Let's go tell them the news". "So have you time to come for lunch with us today or are you rushing off".

"No", said Matthew, "the boy's would love that".

"Come on so," said Patricia.

Matthew got back with Ciaran and Cian at eight o clock they were both asleep in the car. Matthew carried them in home one by one for Perpetual and to their room they took off their shoes and put the duvets over them and left them sleep.

"You're a star Matthew that's what you are", said Mrs. O'Brien. "I didn't know myself for the day it was great".

"Did you get your hair done?" Matthew asked.

"I did", said Perpetual, "do you like it? Shelia took Hanna for the day".

"You look great Perpetual we will have to give you a break more often so we will". Mrs. O'Brien laughed "you'll be sorry you said that".

"No", I won't said, Matthew, "I mean it". "And I have a little news of my own Ormond radio have offered me a talk show of my own I start Sunday for an hour".

"Oh my God", said Mrs. O'Brien that's so exciting.

"Yeah", said Matthew, "but don't tell no one yet I want to see how the first show goes I could be useless and my first could be my last".

"I won't say a word"; said Mrs. O'Brien.

It was Saturday night Matthews garden was thronged he had meant to tell no one but then he thought he would have to tell Shelia when he told Perpetual. And sure then Seorsha was there so he told him too. So when he went home he texted Billy, Fionn, Kevin and Damien. And then he thought I'll ring Catriona because she was so good to call when me and Claire split up. And then he thought he would call Justine and tell her as she had become a good friend of his and Yvonne would hear anyways from her God Father Tom. So they were having a before your first show party and Matthew was delighted his life was in fact now he realized all the better without Claire she would never have liked having all these people around. Too much bother and work. Everybody went home by twelve to let Matthew get a good nights sleep before his big debut, but he was so nervous he couldn't sleep. Justine was outside waiting for Yvonne she was out with the children in Mrs.O'Briens.

"Hey Justine how's about you come in and we have a little drink while you wait?"

"I don't know what's keeping her I texted her a good ten minutes ago and there isn't a sign of her".

"Come in", said Matthew.

"I'll ring Perpetual see what the story is".

Matthew rang the phone was answered straight away he turned to Justine, "she's asleep downstairs can she stay there the night Perpetual wants to know?"

"Yeah sure", said Justine, "I'll head home so".

"Will you not have a quick drink?"

"Go on so", said Justine.

Matthew and Justine sat up talking for hours.

" It's three o clock Matthew", I must go let you get some sleep you are going to be wrecked for your first day.

"Oh my God", said Matthew, "I never felt the time going".

Matthew never slept at eight o clock he got into the shower at nine o clock he walked into the studio Patricia was there waiting for him.

"Oh my god Patricia thank you so much".

"Don't mention it Matthew I'm going to be your anchor woman". "Now its like this I'm going to do all the technical end for you". "This is Turlough he is going to be your producer you've really been thrown in the deep end but don't worry it will all be ok all you have to do is talk and we will take care of the rest I've queued music for you incase anything goes wrong or god forbid its quiet and no one wants to talk to us".

Patricia looked at Matthew he was gone as white as a sheet. "Don't look so worried Matthew you're going to be fine remember all you have to do is talk".

Matthew laughed, "and we have already established I can do that no bother".

"That's it", said Patricia, "it's all going to be fine you will be the number two presenter on this radio".

"Behind you I guess", said Matthew.

"That's it", said Patricia.

"Headphones people", said Turlough.

Matthew and Patricia put on head phones. In five, four, three. The calls started coming in before they were on air.

"Hello", said Matthew.

"Hello this is Miriam".

"Hello Miriam", said Matthew, "how are you?"

"I'm fine not a bother on me".

"And what would you like to talk about today Miriam?"

"Shoes Matthew I know it's not a subject men would be interested in".

"Your ok Miriam go on ahead I know how important shoes are to you women I have an ex wife who was very attached to her shoes when she moved she took them left me behind".

Miriam laughed, "see there's a pair of shoes I love but there 130 euro and I was wondering is it terrible to spend that much on a pair of shoes". "I feel terrible guilty spending that kind of money but I love them".

"Well", said Matthew, "do you work?"

"Yeah".

"And when is the last time you bought yourself anything?"

"I can't remember", said Miriam.

"I say get the shoes Miriam we all deserve a treat if the shoes will bring you a bit of joy have them what harm its your money surely you are entitled to spend it on yourself".

"Oh Miriam we have Sean on the line he wants to talk to you".

"Hi Sean", said Miriam.

"I can't believe you would spend that much money on shoes it's a disgrace and people starving do you know how many people you could feed in Africa with a hundred and thirty euros".

"I suppose", said Miriam.

"Hold on there Sean", said Matthew, "are you not being a bit harsh there like tell me how much did you spend on your car?"

"That's different Matthew I need my car".

"Yeah right, said Matthew go on tell us how much?"

"But Matthew", said Sean, "it's totally different she don't need shoes?"

"Do you know Miriam", Sean?

"No but surely she could do better things with that money pay a bill or something?" "Well Miriam what do you say to that?"

"I don't have much bills Matthew, "I'm only sixteen I live at home".

"Ah Jayus", said Matthew, "you go get your shoes girl you should be ashamed of yourself Sean".

"I didn't know what age she was Matthew".

"Did you have a job at sixteen, Sean?"

"Well", said Matthew.

"No", said Sean.

"There you go Miriam." "Tell us about those shoes".

"Oh I love them Matthew they are three colors red, yellow and grey with a huge buckle". "They are the nicest shoes I've ever seen". "The heel is four and a half inches". "Well they sound great Miriam just be careful you don't break your neck in them they seem very high". "And Miriam you'll enjoy them all the more that you worked for them".

"Thanks ", Matthew.

"Bye now Miriam enjoy your shoes".

"Hello we have Elaine how are you Elaine?"

"Hi Matthew I just want to say Sean is a fool and Miriam your great to be working and your right to get yourself those shoes isn't it way better than going out the weekend and having your money gone and nothing to show for it".

"Thank you Elaine"." Right we will be back with you after these Matthew nodded at Turlough and he put on the commercials". "Jesus Patricia half an hour talking about shoes can you credit it". "Hey Turlough have we these shoes were made for walking on the list".

"I can get it before the ads are over".

"Can we play that straight away when we come back?"

"Yeah no bother".

"You're a pro", said Patricia, told you you'd be fine, its going great.

"It hasn't been bad sure it hasn't".

"Right said Matthew we have Amanda on the line what would you like to talk about Amanda?"

"I just wanted to say I'm delighted you have your own show I love listening to you". "Awe thanks Amanda so how are you?"

"I'm grand".

"And what are you doing this Sunday morning?"

"I'm in bed".

"Oh you should get up your missing some lovely weather".

"Yeah I know my head is killing me though I'm dying".

"A rough night last night was it Amanda?"

"You could say that do you know any good hang over cures?"

"We will throw it open to the listeners Amanda and see if they can help you?"

"Oh Amanda we have Justine on the line for you".

"Is that you our Justine?"

"It is Matthew tell her to get up and go drinking again that will sort it".

"Ha, ha Justine and I'd be as bad as ever tomorrow no anyways the sight of it would make me sick now".

"Oh well thanks for that anyways Justine and thanks for listening in".

"We have Irene next what's your suggestion Irene?"

"She should have tomato juice with Tabasco sauce and a drop of vodka and celery that would sort her".

"Thanks but I've none of those things in the house".

"No luck there either", said Matthew, "well thanks anyways Irene".

"Next we have Rachel what's your suggestion Rachel?"

"Take Solpadine or paracetamol or aspirin or something and drink water".

"That I can do, said Amanda".

"And there I must leave you, said Matthew thank you all for a very enjoyable first show especially Patricia who has sat in studio and held my hand through this whole thing and my brilliant producer Turlough".

10

May brought with it the best weather they had seen in a long time. Matthew's work had all but dried up but the weather was too good to complain or even feel the need to worry. Matthew got up early every morning and he and Perpetual and baby Hanna, and Shelia would go to Dromineer and push Hanna on the swings, they would buy ice cream in the shop. And whilst Shelia and Perpetual would sit out and bask in the sun with baby Hanna taking a nap in her pram Matthew, Kevin, Damien, Billy, Seorsha in between school runs and Liam on occasion would play soccer on the grass at the back. They all wondered how it had been so long since they had made time just to have fun, and hang out. It was heading towards the end of May and the sunshine continued on there were only two weeks left before the fashion show and Matthew spent his time rehearsing they had them dancing and all.

Could this get any more embarrassing Matthew thought?

The show would take hours as there were variety acts in between and local designers were also showing their work, and first there would be the wine and cheese reception. Yvonne had asked Matthew if he could get them some male models on the first nights rehearsal as a lot of the men who had promised had forgotten got busy or were too embarrassed to go through with it. Matthew had rang and roped Kevin, Billy Damien, Liam, Fionn and Seorsha into it. Catriona, Adrian, Amelda and Tom were at the fashion show to. It wasn't too bad they actually had great craic and spent all their evenings for the two weeks in the pub laughing. Justine was down with the other transition year mothers making sure everything was going smoothly so there was a huge gang of them every night.

"I'll be sorry when this is over" Matthew said to Justine, "I've gotten used to you being around". "I really enjoy talking to you".

"Its nice having you to talk to too", said Justine, "well this time next week it will be all over".

"Can I give you a lift home", asked Matthew.

"That would be great, said Justine.

Matthew dropped Justine to her apartment. They have the light and all on for you, said Matthew.

"So they have", said Justine. "Tony must have fallen asleep drunk up there again".

Justine climbed the stairs to the apartment expecting Tony to be asleep drunk on the chair in front of the telly. She was surprised when she turned the key in the door and was not greeted by the stomach turning smell of stale drink emanating from every pore in Tony's body. She was even more surprised to see that there were a bunch of red roses on the table. She walked over and noticed the page sitting on the table in front of the flowers. She looked down and read it. I'm sorry but I've left you I've gone to England you'll understand in time. I won't be back. Enjoy the flowers. Justine burst out laughing and she couldn't understand it. I should be crying she kept thinking to herself. Yvonne walked in the door

"Mam what's so funny?"

"He's gone pet Tony he's gone to England he says he won't be back".

"Oh thank God mam thank God", said Yvonne.

"Come on, said Justine linking Yvonne under the arm we are going to get all dressed up and go out somewhere".

"But man it's twelve o' clock where will be open?"

"We will go have a Chinese", said Justine.

"Mam can we get it take away and have a bottle of wine they won't serve me in the restaurant".

"Of course we can pet", said Justine, "but we won't be making a habit of you drinking this is only because we are celebrating".

The following day Yvonne and Justine bought paint and painted the whole apartment. "This is great", said Yvonne, "it's brilliant".

Her excitement was at fever pitch the fashion show was on the end of the week and she was turning fifteen. They were just finishing putting up border in the sitting room when the door opened and an estate agent walked in with a young couple.

"As you can see this will be the perfect first home for you".

He stopped in his tracks when he saw Justine and Yvonne.

"It is customary to be out of the premises when it is being viewed", he said to Justine. "I'm sure it is she said but you are in the wrong apartment this apartment is not for sale".

He turned to the couple could you wait outside a minute. Then to Yvonne he said "your landlord informed you weeks ago and told you to be moved out by now". "I will have to inform him you are still here".

"My landlord and who would that be?" asked Justine. Yvonne walked out the door.

"Tony Stewart".

"Tony was is my ex partner". "Whilst the apartment is in his name it is my business that pays the mortgage and I say it's not for sale".

"It's all the one what you say". "The paper work is in order, Tony informed us of his intention to sell six weeks ago". "You will have to be out by the end of this week".

"I will be contacting Tony once I get back to the office and telling him how you're still occupying the premises".

He walked out the door to the couple.

"Would you like to come in and look around any questions I'll answer them".

Justine grabbed her bag and walked out. She didn't know what she was going to do. She didn't know where to turn she took out her mobile and rang the first person she thought of Matthew. Matthew was putting a baby swing on the swing set for Hanna when his mobile rang.

"Justine how's things you all ready for rehearsal tonight not long left now".

Justine began to cry.

"Justine what's wrong", said Matthew.

"Tony left he's gone to England".

"Oh Justine I'm so sorry but believe me it's not the end of the world I know how you're feeling".

"Matthew", Justine interrupted him it's not that he is gone I'm glad he is gone it's that he is selling the apartment over our heads and I don't know what to do".

"Where are you Justine", said Matthew, "I'm coming to get you'.

"I'm just walking I'm across from Cakes and things".

"Right", said Matthew, go in there and wait for me". "I'll meet you in ten minutes".

"Is everything ok", asked Mrs. O'Brien.

"No", said Matthew, "its Justine". "Tony's gone and he is selling the roof from over her head her and Yvonne have nowhere to go". "I'm going to bring them back here".

"I'll go in and make up two rooms for you which two will I do?"

"Any two you like", said Matthew. "Your great", Perpetual, "I'll finish the swing once I get back".

Perpetual called Shelia and the two women went in to Matthews to make the beds. "Never a dull moment", said Shelia.

"I'm very fond of Justine and Yvonne they are lovely", said Mrs. O'Brien. "I'd love to see Matthew and Justine get together.

"I hope they come now", said Shelia.

"Ah", said Perpetual, "what's for him won't pass him".

Matthew arrived at Cakes and Things and walked through to the back Justine sat there with a cup of coffee and one sat opposite her for Matthew. Matthew walked up and sat down beside her.

"Now Justine", Matthew began before Justine got a chance to talk, "don't you be worrying this is a terrible situation but if this is the way things are and there is nothing you can do about it then there is only one thing to be done me and you are going back to that apartment we are going to pack all your stuff and you and Yvonne will come stay with me until you can find some where suitable". "I would love the company". "It's a five bed roomed house there is loads of room everybody will have as much space as they want". "Now come on drink up that coffee and we'll start loading the cars". "Between yours and mine we will do it in a few runs".

"Oh Matthew that's to much we couldn't do that I just wanted someone to talk to I wasn't expecting you to fix everything".

"No argument", said Matthew, "until you find somewhere suitable your coming with me".

Justine threw her arms around Matthew, "now to find Yvonne she said".

"Why", said Matthew, "where is she?

"She walked out when we were told we were homeless".

Justine rang Yvonne's mobile but it never answered.

"Here", said Matthew, "let me".

Matthew rang Yvonne's mobile and she answered it.

"Where are you Yvonne?" Matthew asked.

"I'm at the bus stop".

"And what on earth are you doing there?"

"What about this fashion show you bullied half the town into are you just going to disappear and not bother with it, walk out on the lot of us?"

"No", said Yvonne.

"Stay where you are I'm on my way up to you I have something to tell you".

"Where you going anyway?"

"I don't know", said Yvonne.

Matthew got up from the table, "be back in a minute Justine". Matthew walked up the street and around the corner to Yvonne.

"I hear your homeless he said".

"That's not funny", said Yvonne.

"I know that", said Matthew. "How's about this you and your mam come stay with me until you can find somewhere".

"I don't know", said Yvonne, "no offence to you but I don't want to I'm sick of moving, I don't want to go nowhere".

"You'll be right beside baby Hanna you can play with her whenever you want". "I can give you the ensuite". "You'll have your own telly with all the channels". "Come on Yvonne we are wasting time we could be packing". "What do you say I promise you it will be ok and I'll talk to your mam your next move will be your last promise".

"Ok", said Yvonne they both walked down to Cakes and Things, to Justine.

"Do you want anything", asked Matthew?

"Nah", said Yvonne I'm good when we moving?

"Tonight no time like the present".

"So it's ok with you", said Justine.

"Have I any choice", said Yvonne.

"Yvonne drives a hard bargain", said Matthew.

"She is having the downstairs ensuite". "Come on and we will get started he winked at Justine".

They only needed the one run. All Yvonne's stuff fitted in one black bag. Justine had four black bags and two boxes with photographs and nick nacks. They were pulling into Matthews drive at nine o clock. Shelia and Perpetual were out front waiting to welcome them to the street.

"Thanks", said Yvonne.

"Matthew can I go next door and play with the kids".

"If it's ok with your mam and Perpetual", said Matthew.

"Its fine by me", said Mrs. O'Brien.

"What about unpacking?" Justine asked.

"Ah let her off", said Matthew, "she can do that tomorrow".

Matthew carried in the stuff he left Yvonne's black bag inside her room door. He went upstairs to Justine and told her if she wanted any help to give him a call. He went down stairs and opened a bottle of wine. Perpetual arrived in.

"I have a minute Yvonne has the kids do you want a hand with anything?"

"No, everything is ok Jesus, Perpetual said Matthew they don't possess ten bags full of stuff between them".

"Some people don't need a lot of material things Matthew". "You can only wear one thing at a time".

"No Perpetual I'd say it tells the story of many a move in hurried circumstances".

"You never know do you?"

"I guess not", said Mrs. O'Brien, "but it all comes down to how people want to live". "Like why do people suffer over and over again it's because Matthew they are happy in their suffering". "When people decide to be happy they will it's like that saying why people suffer because they haven't yet suffered enough". "Look Justine and Yvonne are happy they are happy to have a roof over their heads". "They are happy to have you as a friend". "They are good people and I don't like to say this but I think that they will bring a happiness and laughter to your house that it never had". "Claire had everything yet it was no good to her cause she was constantly looking for drama because she sought her happiness in misery some people are just like that Matthew". "But Justine she has her daughter she has started her own business she is a good woman she is trying to make her world better". "She is the type of person who will do you the world of good". "She is the type of woman I would like to see you with".

Matthew laughed, "for Christ's sake don't say that to her you'll frighten her off".

They laughed. Justine came down the stairs.

"I heard the laughing is it ok if I join ye?"

"Of course", said Matthew, "you don't have to ask here have a glass of wine".

Yvonne walked in the door with Hanna in her arms, "the boys are gone to bed Mrs. O'Brien can they watch the chipmunks in bed?"

"Your very good Yvonne thanks yeah I find they fall asleep ten minutes in to it anyways".

"Will I put Hanna down now?"

"Oh Yvonne", said Mrs. O'Brien, "can you come move in with me?"

Yvonne laughed and went back to Perpetual's with Hanna.

"What age is she Justine", asked Perpetual?

"Fifteen next week, the years are flying".

"We will have to have a party", said Matthew.

"There is no need for that", said Justine.

"Justine", said Mrs. O'Brien, "can I ask you what age are you?"

"I'm thirty one".

"God your great do you know Matthew is the same age as you?"

"Oh right", said Justine, "I knew we were in or around the same age".

"Well", said Mrs. O'Brien, "I'll head out send your little girl back in to you".

Yvonne walked in the door. "Matthew can I have a shower".

"You don't have to ask", said Matthew.

"Justine will you show her, her room Yvonne I hope you will treat here as your home while you are here sleep well".

Justine came back they both spent until the sun was rising talking. Matthew had never had a night like this before he told her how he had met Claire how he and Dave had met their first day of secondary school, about Fas college and being a builder. She told him all about having Yvonne the numerous counties they had lived in. And they laughed all night Matthew felt a great peace within himself. He could let go all bitterness towards Dave and Claire they were just other people other faces they didn't matter. They heard Yvonne get up it was only seven o clock.

"You didn't stay up all night did you?"

"Why you up so early asked Justine?"

"I'm going to make breakfast I'm going to walk down to Tesco to get shopping".

"We can have our first family meal together".

"Yvonne we're not Matthew's family we are guests don't be saying things like that". "Sorry Matthew", said Yvonne.

"Don't be said Matthew while you are here I'd like you to think of us as family if that's ok with you Justine?"

"Its perfect Matthew", said Yvonne.

Justine laughed.

"Come on", said Matthew, "how's about we go down town to the café let some one else cook our first breakfast".

They got in Matthew's car and drove to the restaurant and had their breakfast. When Matthew went up to pay Justine had got their before him. He was shocked Claire in years of dating and one year of marriage had never done anything like that.

He went back down to the table "there was no need for that", he said.

"Yes there was", said Justine, "we want to show our appreciation".

"You will have to stay for good at this rate", said Matthew.

Justine asked Matthew to drop her of at the travel agents on the way up home. She was going to go in do what she had to and go up to Matthew's to bed.

"Is that ok with you Matthew", she asked.

"Of course it is" Matthew replied. "My home is our home now and I'm so glad of the company".

"Thanks", said Justine. "Are you coming with me Yvonne?"

"I have to get my uniform for school". "Can I come up home with you Matthew and change?"

"Of course you can", said Matthew.

"Don't be bothering Matthew Yvonne he wants to go to bed you can come to work with me for the day go in to school tomorrow".

"But the fashion show", said Yvonne, "I want to go in".

"That's enough", said Justine.

"It's no bother", said Matthew, "I have no work I've nothing to do I'll bring Yvonne up home with me she can change I'll drop her to school and then I'll collect you and we can both go up home together". "Will you have what you have to do done in an hour and a half?"

"Yeah I will", said Justine, "but I don't want to be putting you out".

"Your not", said Matthew.

Justine got out and Yvonne went to get into the front.

"You'll stay in the back and keep your safety belt on", said Yvonne, "you've got to be sixteen to sit in the front and you're not even fifteen".

Matthew took Yvonne up home dropped her to school collected Justine and they both went to their rooms and slept.

It was the night of the fashion show the hall was packed. There was a walk way going right around the hall and down the middle. The dj and his mixing desk stood in the middle of the hall. Back stage the nerves paralyzed everyone. Yvonne was delighted she had never done anything exciting for her birthday, she looked at the fashion show as her party. Up home Shelia and Perpetual decorated Matthew's sitting room with balloons. Maria arrived over with the birthday cake from "the Cakes we bake" confectioners in town.

"Jesus", said Shelia, "they spelled Yvonne wrong they left out an N".

"Yvonne wont mind", said Perpetual.

Seorsha brought down his present a voucher for one of the teen clothes shops in town. Perpetual and Shelia were giving Yvonne cards with twenty euro inside. Seorsha go collect Emmet will you the hall is being locked for ten they will be home before we know it. Yvonne walked up to Matthew your very quiet Yvonne.

"Nobody has come", she said.

"What do you mean", said Matthew, "the hall is full?"

"Yeah but Emmet, Mrs. O'Brien, Shelia, Seorsha the kids they never came they are not here".

"They could be here but you can't see them".

"No", said Yvonne, "I walked around the hall they aren't here".

"This isn't really their thing pet".

"But I organized it I wanted them here".

"Ah Yvonne don't let it upset you enjoy your night trust me you won't be disappointed".

The show started at six and finished at nine. Yvonne was exhausted when it was over. Justine Matthew and Yvonne drove home. Yvonne had forgotten all about her birthday when they pulled up to the house and she saw the banner in front of the house happy birthday Yvonne she jumped out of the car and screamed.

The following morning Matthew got up to clean the house after Yvonne's birthday party, he walked downstairs and the house sparkled before him. Yvonne was asleep on the couch. He smiled and turned to go back up stairs.

Yvonne sat up on the couch. "Matthew thanks for my party".

"Your welcome pet", said Matthew. "Was it you who cleaned the house?"

"Yeah", said Yvonne, "I wanted to say thanks for all this". "It's nice to be here Matthew".

"Its nice to have you both", said Matthew. "How's about we all go out for dinner tonight like the three of us what do you think?"

"Ah Matthew there's no need to be throwing money away". "Why don't I cook us something and we can watch a dvd?"

"No", said Matthew, "I want us to do something together for your birthday".

"It's settled".

"Right", said Yvonne, "I better get ready for school".

"Well only if you want to your mother and me were talking last night and we decided that you deserve a day off after all its Friday".

"Oh nice one I'm going back to bed".

"Me too", said Matthew.

Justine was going into the bathroom as Matthew was going back up the stairs to bed. "You won't believe this Justine, Yvonne stayed up all night cleaning the house imagine she's a great little girl".

"I don't often hear that", said Justine, "yeah she seems really happy here".

"Happy and settled", said Matthew, "oh well I'm going back to bed". "Yvonne is gone to bed and what are you doing?"

"Oh", said Justine, "I'm going to work the joys".

"I am taking us out to dinner tonight me you and Yvonne", said Matthew.

"You are in your hole", said Justine, "you've already done more than enough for us". "No arguments", said Matthew, "it's settled".

"What time do you finish work?" I'm off at six.

"Will eight o clock be good for you we will go to "The Place to Unwind".

"That's so expensive Matthew".

"Yeah maybe but I want to eat there and I want company surely you don't want to disappoint me".

"You're too good", said Justine, she leaned in towards Matthew and kissed him. Matthew pulled back. Justine turned red walked into the bathroom and locked the door. Matthew went into his bedroom and got back into bed.

What have I done? What have I done?

Justine asked herself as she cleansed her face showered went to work all day while she was in work. She dreaded the thought of going back to Matthew's and she didn't want to have to tell Yvonne. Matthew might be uncomfortable around them now. Maybe he would want them out.

Shit, shit, shit thought Justine I am so stupid why did I do that?

Matthew lay in bed thinking. I wonder am I reading too much into this kiss it felt so nice though. Why did I have to pull away though I'm such a fool. Maybe she would come on a date with me but then if it was only a friendly kiss she would be uncomfortable if I ask her and she might move out? Oh what will I do?? There was a knock on the door.

"Is that you Yvonne?"

"Yeah I have tea and toast for you it's half twelve".

"Jesus, said Matthew you have to be messing?"

"No it is".

"I was just lying here awake thinking I didn't realize that was the time".

"What were you thinking about", asked Yvonne. "I bet I know you fancy me mam right?"

"Why do you say that?"

"Because I know I see the way you look at each other'. "I'm right I know I am".

"If you were right how would you feel about it".

"Oh go for it", said Yvonne, "I don't mind".

"Are you sure", said Matthew?

"Yeah certain", you ask her out. "I'll stay at home tonight and you ask her at dinner".

"Are you sure you're sure?"

"Certain".

"You're great Yvonne".

"I know", said Yvonne laughing.

Justine's stomach was tied in knots all day oh my God I hope he doesn't want us out. Matthew had showered and shaved he had sent Yvonne to the shop to get him a bunch of flowers.

"Red rose's yeah .red roses Yvonne a hundred of them".

"That's too much Matthew its stupid".

"Do you think she won't like them?"

"Course she will like them but she would like an ordinary bunch just as well".

"No, no Yvonne if she says yes it will be our first date get the hundred".

"Ok so", said Yvonne, "I'll be back in a while".

"Here's fifty euros get yourself something".

"I don't need anything", said Yvonne, "I'm good".

"I know your good just take it".

"No Matthew honestly I'll be back in a minute".

Claire was home before Yvonne.

"Where is Yvonne, Matthew", she asked as she walked in the door?

"Gone to the shop she'll be back in a minute can I talk to you?"

"Go on", said Justine, "I just want to say about this morning".

"Oh please Justine let me go first".

"Ok Matthew".

"I really like you Justine I think you're a sound girl I'd love for us to be more than friends I was wondering if we could treat tonight as our first date?"

"Oh yes Matthew of course yes, yes".

Yvonne walked in the door with the roses.

"Why you crying mam you didn't say no did you?"

"Oh so you told her first", said Justine, "the two of you honestly your thick as thieves".

11

Every Sunday Matthew had his radio show. Building had picked up he worked three days a week doing carpentry unless he was doing a favor for a friend. He and all his friends had become so much closer and he was so much happier with Justine. He was surprised how he had not felt too badly the pinch of being left with such a huge loan to repay. It was November and Yvonne and Matthew and Justine were sitting at the table eating their breakfast when Ciaran ran in the door crying. It's nanny she's on the floor and she won't get up.

"Yvonne call the ambulance", said Matthew, "he and Justine ran in next door".

"Ciaran, get Shelia and Seorsha".

Perpetual was on the floor in the kitchen. Matthew knelt down beside Perpetual and lowered his ear to her mouth and felt her breath on his face he but his hand on her wrist and felt her pulse.

"Justine its slow 40 but its there".

Yvonne walked in the door and told them the ambulance was on its way.

"Can you take the kids out home honey", said Justine.

Yvonne went upstairs woke Cian and took Hanna from her cot and they went out home. Ciaran arrived in with Seorsha and Shelia.

"Go out to Yvonne Ciaran", said Matthew.

"Will she be ok Matthew?"

"The ambulance is on its way Ciaran we will know more then". "Go out to Yvonne as soon as I know anything I'll let you know".

Ciaran left and as he went into Yvonne he could hear the sirens. The paramedics took Perpetual to the hospital. Shelia went in the ambulance with her, Justine, Matthew, and Seorsha followed behind in Seorsha's car. They enquired at the reception of the casualty department when they went in and were told that Perpetual had been taken straight through and as soon as she had been examined by the doctor they would let them through. They sat for what seemed like an eternity in the waiting room.

Justine turned to Matthew, "if there is anything wrong with her what will happen those kids?"

"I don't know", said Matthew.

"Matthew I don't like to say this really like it's your house but if anything is wrong could we take them?"

Matthew hugged Justine, "I was thinking the same but I didn't like to say and it's not my house it's our house you know I'd marry you in the morning if I could".

Justine kissed Matthew. Seorsha was coming in from parking the car.

"Jesus you two", he said, "go get a room do ye ever stop Jesus".

They laughed. "She's gone straight through once the doctor's seen her they will come get us".

They sat in silence staring at the door waiting to be called. Justine nudged Matthew and Seorsha she saw Shelia's head appear around the door. They got up and went in.

"The doctor wants to talk with us all", said Shelia.

They walked after Shelia into a tiny cubical Perpetual was awake and holding cotton wool to her arm where they had taken blood.

"You gave us all a fright", said Seorsha, "how you feeling?"

The doctor appeared around the curtain before Perpetual could answer.

"What was it doctor", asked Matthew?

"It's exhaustion at eighty six it's a lot to be raising three kids and one is only a year I believe?" "Oh my god", said Matthew, Shelia, Justine and Seorsha together.

"Perpetual we had no idea you were in your eighties my god" said Seorsha.

"Anyway", said the doctor. "It's exhaustion Perpetual will have to take things easy". "We'd like to keep her here for a while but I'm afraid all we can offer is a trolley there are no beds".

"Can she come home with us", said Justine we have the room.

"Yes that would be great and the minor children?"

"They are with us already".

"No, no, Matthew Justine I couldn't possible put you out like that I just couldn't".

"Don't be daft", said Matthew, "your coming with us and that's it, it will be great to have that barn of a house full".

"That would be great", said the doctor, "we have done some routine tests but I'm not expecting anything to show up in them Perpetual hasn't been eating her blood sugar dropped too busy taking care of others to take care of herself".

The doctor turned to Perpetual "a week's total bed rest you hear?"

"Seorsha", said Justine calling him over to the side, "will you go out ring Yvonne and tell her to move her stuff up to one of the bedrooms upstairs and to get the kids clothes and move them in upstairs too". "Tell her not to worry about moving a cot for Hanna I have one already put away and I'll collect it on the way home.

"Oh my god Justine I'm so happy for ye".

"Sush", said Justine", "I've told no one yet, not even Matthew".

"I won't say a word", said Seorsha.

"Grand", said Matthew, "can we head now so?"

"Yes said the doctor we will get a porter to take Perpetual out you can go be bringing up the car".

"Thanks doctor", said Perpetual.

"Your welcome", said the doctor.

"We won't all fit", said Seorsha.

"Matthew you take Aunty Shelia with you and Perpetual, and Justine and I will get a taxi back" said Seorsha.

"Are you sure", said Matthew?

"Yeah definite".

"Ok so".

When Matthew, Perpetual, and Shelia walked into the house, Maria and Anna were there they were helping Yvonne move everything. They had the room downstairs all ready for Perpetual. Sheila and Matthew helped her into the room and Anna and Maria helped her into bed. Justine and Seorsha went to the nursery shop on the way home and collected the cot.

"Can you take it up to yours until I tell Matthew, this wasn't planned I don't know how he is going to take it", said Justine.

"You need have no worries there Justine", said Seorsha, he will be over the moon, a new baby on the street this will be great".

They got the taxi to drop them to Seorsha's house he took in the cot and Justine went in home.

"Oh there you are love", said Matthew.

"Can I talk to you a minute in the kitchen", Justine looked worried.

Oh shit thought Matthew it's all too much for her she's leaving.

He followed her into the room.

"Matthew I don't know how to say this so I'm going to come straight out with it I'm pregnant, its yours I'm eleven weeks I went to the doctor last week it's yours I'll do any test ..."

"Matthew kissed her on the lips stopping her mid stream why did you look worried this is good news can we tell everyone?"

"Yeah why not", said Justine, "why not".

Mrs. O'Brien was anxious and despite great effort she insisted on going home after a week. All the neighbors made an effort to take the kids more. Every day at Justine and Matthews's insistence they had their dinner with them. Hanna was growing up she was walking and talking now. Not a baby any more but a little girl. Mrs. O'Brien worried what would become of them if anything happened her? The end of June Justine gave birth to another little girl they called her Triona. Mrs. O'Brien called in to see her the day she came home.

"Mrs. O'Brien", said Justine, "we have been meaning to talk to you about something for a while".

"Oh what is it she asked?"

"We were wondering", said Matthew if it would be ok with you we would like to become legal guardians to your three just make things official if ever they would need to come to live with us".

"And we are not suggesting in any way that anything is going to happen any time soon you could see us all out", said Justine.

"Oh thank God", said Perpetual, it's been a worry to me always to be honest but especially since I collapsed there last winter". "Your so good are you sure you've got a family of your own".

"We are both certain", said Justine.

"Yeah", said Matthew, "we wouldn't want it any other way". "After this ones christening so", said Matthew, "I'll get on to my solicitor and he can sort out what we will have to do".

"Oh that's such a weight off my mind", said Mrs. O'Brien, "you will never know how much this means to me".

12

Every morning Claire got up and went to work for six am, every morning except Sunday. Her days merged into a blur with no end and no beginning. When Claire would later look back on her three years in New York the first few weeks were etched vividly in her mind the excitement and buzz and the joy of anticipation in it all. But from the night they first moved into the apartment her days merged into a blur of hours her only definite memory her tired sore feet that walked thankless miles across a diner floor. They ate off Claire's money paid the bills off Claire's money and Claire even managed to amaze herself by being able to pay for another years rent in advance from the tips jar that she kept hidden in work. Dave hung around recording studios or else sat at home watching television or else was on line, and hung out at the bar on the corner in the evenings where he met up and became friends with Trent the owner. The basement of the bar was empty and spacious. Dave often heard people rapping dancing and singing in the park across the street. One day he decided to ask Trent if he could open a club in the basement. At first Trent was reluctant he was afraid that a club would bring trouble and his bar was quiet and he wanted to keep it that way. Dave true to form wasn't long talking Trent into it and before long Dave was hiring interior designers. The end result was amazing. The seating was large blush purple velvet sofas that seated up to six. There were two white marble tables to each sofa. The bar was entirely made of white marble and the floor was white and all the walls were mirrored glass save one. Claire looked around the club in awe.

"Jesus Dave you've done a great job, how many will fit in here?"

"The fire department has only cleared us for 550 people".

It's enough though Claire.

"I'm looking to create an exclusive atmosphere". "I'm setting up a web site for the club; people will be able to watch themselves on line the next day". "I'm going to have rap battles and all here I see those kids out in the park, I might even get to manage one of them and the little bastard will make me rich". "I'm not wasting money on a dj either I've downloaded thousand of music files to my computer for free". "The ceiling is low I'll be able to hook up the computer to the speakers and it will work fine". "I'll even let the little thugs bring in their own beats and I'll use them". "All for nothing". "This place will run itself".

"I see said Claire do you not think that you might be a little under qualified for that". "Like I mean do you not think that to get involved in this you would at least have to like hip hop music and the people who perform it". "And you can't rap you can't sing". "What would you know about battling? It's a good idea but you would want to get in someone who has a clue like a well known DJ to run the place for you, it would attract the kids too". "And you can't be using illegal down loads you'll be fined or worse". The room suddenly started to spin Claire felt like she was falling down a tunnel. It was dark when Claire woke up on the floor her neck felt stiff she forced herself to push herself up from the floor. She could see a pair of legs sitting opposite her.

"Look at the state of my floor after you".

Dave threw a cloth and bottle of spray detergent at Claire.

"Clean up that mess and in future stay out of my business".

Claire put her hand to her head there was dry blood stuck to her hair. Have I been here long?

"Yeah your lazy ass been lying there all day clean up that mess and get out of here you're an embarrassment to me the state of you go clean yourself up".

Claire walked out the door of the club she felt dizzy and disorientated the daylight blinded her and her head was splitting with a headache. She didn't know where she was, she didn't realize she was in the middle of the road until the horns started blowing.

"Get of the road", people roared she felt someone's arms around here lifting her off the road.

"Matthew?" she called.

"It's me Shawn your ok I met you when you first moved here".

Claire looked puzzled Shawn felt something sticky and warm under his hand he looked down his fingers were covered in blood.

"Sweet Jesus Claire you've been hit we've got to get you to hospital".

Shawn lifted Claire up in his arms and carried her into the escalade and laid her on the back seat. He drove her to the nearest hospital and carried her in his arms into the accident and emergency department. Claire had lost consciousness as he carried her in the door. Suddenly there was a huge rush of people Shawn was asked a thousand questions he could not answer. Claire's address he didn't know.

"I met her when she arrived in New York three years ago I drove her from the airport". "I remember her because she knows my Irish relations".

"Sir has she any allergies".

"I don't know", said Shawn, "like I told you".

"Yeah, yeah we know", replied the doctor asking Shawn the questions.

"We have to rush her to theatre she is losing a lot of blood it appears her spleen is ruptured". "What happened her can you tell us".

"I came across her wandering around in the middle of the traffic I was going into work from home that's all I know".

"Has she any family you can contact for her?" "I'm afraid she is quiet ill".

"I don't know", said Shawn, "I could go try and find her boyfriend who she came over here with I have a vague memory of the area they are living in".

"That would be great said the doctor can I just get you to sign the consent for surgery in proxy as we need to proceed immediately".

Shawn hesitated he didn't know Claire to be singing anything. A nurse came out and whispered in the doctor's ear.

"One moment sir", said the doctor, "could we ask you to go to the waiting room with this nurse it appears we have obtained phone consent from her husband in Ireland his number was found in her wallet and we took a chance and called it". "We will need you to answer a few questions nothing serious".

"Yeah no problem", said Shawn, "but like I told you I was on my way to work so I'll have to head soon".

Shawn followed the nurse to a small room to the side. Shawn was left all alone in the room fifteen minutes later the door opened and two NYPD officers walked in. Shawn was surprised he couldn't think what they wanted with him. There was a male and female officer.

"Sir asked the female officer we need to ask you a few questions in relation to the lady you brought into the A&E department today".

"What is your relationship to this woman?"

"I met her when I drove her and her boyfriend from JFK airport to the hotel they were staying in when they came to New York first".

"When was that", asked the male officer?"

"It was a long time ago now I can't rightly remember but maybe two three years".

"What do you do for a living Sir, asked the female officer?"

"I drive for a limousine company".

"And, said the female officer you expect us to believe that you remember a woman that you drove once from the airport three years ago".

"I drove them twice her and her partner once to the hotel and to their apartment when they moved in".

"Can you explain to us the injuries on this woman who you have brought to A&E today?"

"I don't know I found her in the middle of traffic maybe she got hit".

"Cuff him we'll bring him down town".

"What", said Shawn, "I've done nothing, you can't do this I want a lawyer".

"If you're so innocent what do you need a lawyer for?" asked the female officer, "we are arresting you under suspicion of assault of Claire Ryan she read him his rights". Shawn was brought down to the nearest station. He was stripped and searched his shoe laces and belt were taken and he was locked in a cell.

"As you have requested a Lawyer we must wait for one to come before we question you" an officer informed him.

It was the following morning when Shawn was brought from the cell and questioned. He was brought into a room with a table and four chairs. A man with a brief case approached him.

"Have you been ill treated in anyway?"

"No", said Shawn, "I haven't but I got no phone call my wife I wasn't home last night she'll be worried sick".

Two men in suits entered the room.

"Excuse me", said the solicitor, "why was my client not granted a phone call". "I ask that he be immediately granted this right after which I am to be given fifteen minutes privacy with my client".

"Check the log", said the detective to the other officer with him, "I am sure my co-workers offered this man a phone call he obviously declined".

Five minutes later an officer in uniform returned.

"It is recorded that a phone call was offered and declined and it is signed by the accused".

"The solicitor looked at the entry"

"Is that your signature Shawn?"

Shawn looked at the signature Shawn Johnson.

"That's not my signature"

"I will have to ask you to allow me time with my client".

"Fifteen minutes", said the detective.

The two men withdrew from the room.

"I swear to you said Shawn I did nothing, I found her wandering around in the traffic I saw blood I brought her to hospital I swear I did nothing".

"And your signature are you sure you were not offered a phone call?"

"Yes", said Shawn, "that's not my signature it doesn't even remotely resemble it".

"Is there anything I should know before they start to question you?"

"No", said Shawn, "apart from the odd parking violation I have nothing to tell".

"I don't understand this". "I have read the file, said the solicitor". "Apart from the fact you brought this woman to hospital there is nothing to indicate that you have been guilty of any wrong doing". "Your car however has been swabbed and large traces of blood and hair were found in the back".

"I brought her to hospital in the back of that car that's why".

"I know that said the solicitor I'm just saying if you want me to help you, you have to tell me everything". "This woman I believe is in a very serious condition if she dies this all becomes very serious".

"I did nothing to her".

The detectives entered the room.

"Are we ready to begin?"

The detective pressed a button and the camera began recording. The detectives showed Shawn photos that had been taken the previous day in A&E. The detectives took one look at Shawn's face when he saw the photo's and knew this was not their man he looked as though he could get sick. The solicitor and detectives exchanged a look.

"Oh my God", said Shawn. "Oh my God".

"A full MRI has been performed there are over twenty old fractures multiple stab wounds". "You can see from the photos..."

Shawn cut across the officer, "what are they?"

"They are presumed to be cigarette burns".

"How, how could someone do this?"

"Can you give any explanation for this?"

"I don't know this woman only to see, and I can tell you by talking to her you would have no idea that this was going on". "I had nothing to do with this".

"Are you going to charge my client or release him?"

"We will release him on his own recognizance once we are finished questioning him". "Can you tell us of anyone who you think might be responsible for this?"

"I don't like to accuse anyone I don't know them that well".

"Know who that well?"

"She lives with her partner boyfriend Dave I don't know their address but she works at the All American diner I can show you where it is".

Dave was in the basement trying to hook up speakers to the computer. He had never looked for Claire even though he was aware she was missing since the previous night. *She'll come home before long she has no money she has no where to go, he thought.* "Come on so", Mr. Johnson said the detective, "lead the way".

"If you are taking my client with you I'm coming to", said the solicitor.

The two detectives and Shawn and the solicitor walked into the diner.

"I've been looking for you Shawn", said Jamine.

"I heard that you picked up our Claire yesterday?" "What happened her how is she?" "I called up to Dave but got no answer". "I know it must be serious this is the first time in three years she hasn't been in".

"Jamine", said Shawn, "these are detectives this is a solicitor terrible injuries have been inflicted on Claire and not just today over a long period of time". "I was arrested because I took her to hospital yesterday they think it's me".

"That's ridiculous", said Jamine.

"They want to see Dave do you know where he is?"

"Yeah", said Jamine, "and I also know that it is far more likely that he is the one you want", Jamine said to the officers.

"I'll take you down there, he's opening a club in the basement of The Ramblers Rest". So Shawn, Jamine the two detectives and the solicitor walked in the door of the basement of the club that was never to be. Dave looked up from the laptop in surprise. "What is it?"

The detectives walked over to Dave.

"Can we ask you your name Sir?"

"Dave Danaher".

"Are you familiar with one Claire Ryan?"

"Yeah", said Dave, "what's she done now?"

"She's in hospital we are afraid Sir", said one of the detectives.

The other detective had been walking around the club. He called the other man over. They looked at the floor there were tiny broken glass fragments on the floor and a bottle of detergent and cloth.

"Were you cleaning up a mess over here sir?"

"No", said Dave, "Claire was she is the clumsiest person I know".

Dave took a cigarette from a pack and went to light it.

"Are we upsetting you Sir", asked one of the detectives, "are you nervous?"

"No", said Dave, "why would I be nervous?"

"We are just going to get forensics down?"

"You won't find Claire's blood if that's what you're looking"

"Why would we be looking for Claire's blood?"

"I just thought when you said she'd been assaulted..."

"We never said she'd been assaulted, we said she was in hospital".

"Why would you presume she was assaulted sir".

Dave turned to run he tore towards the light that streamed in the doorway. Jamine stuck out his foot as Dave passed him and Dave came crashing down on the floor. The two detectives cuffed Dave and pulled him to his feet.

It was a summer's day Yvonne was home from work Emmet was with her. Matthew and Justine were out in the lawn setting the large fold out tables Liam had leant them for their barbeque. Shelia and Perpetual sat on deck chairs under the cherry tree and Ciaran and Cian played football. Fionn, Kevin, Liam, Billy, Damien and Seorsha carried extra chairs through the house to the garden. Melanie Jane and Amanda sat sipping glasses of wine. Hanna sat on the rug in the shade playing with one year old Triona.

"They are like sisters" Justine whispered to Matthew.

He laughed, "yeah and the boys are brilliant with her".

Yvonne walked over and sat down on the rug with the two little girls Ciaran and Cian walked over and sat down beside them.

"The solicitor's here said Catriona as she walked into the garden with a big cake".

They all gathered around as Justine and Matthew signed the form making them the legal guardians to Cian, Ciaran and

Hanna. The phone was ringing Yvonne ran in and answered it. She came out to get Matthew she looked pale.

"It's a hospital in America they are ringing about Claire".

Matthew took the phone in his hand.

"Hello?"

"Are you the husband of Claire Ryan?"

"I am but we are separated over three years". "You should contact her partner Dave that's if they are still together this is nothing to do with me".

"Sir it's very important your wife I mean Claire needs emergency surgery or she may die we are trying to obtain consent the quickest way possible are you willing to give consent?"

"Yeah, yeah", said Matthew.

"Also your ex wife has no insurance".

"I will give you my details you can bill me here in Ireland", said Matthew, "do whatever is necessary".

"Thank you sir I will put you on to administration and they will take your details". Matthew walked back out onto the lawn and over to Justine.

"You did the right thing Matthew giving consent but paying her bills surely Dave should do that they got enough out of you".

"I know", said Matthew, "I just don't know what to do".

"Don't worry", said Justine, "lets enjoy this evening and tomorrow we will contact the hospital see what the story is".

"Whatever has to be done", said Justine, "we will face it together".

"Let's say nothing about this to anyone yet", Matthew said to Justine. "Today is a big day for the children I don't want to spoil it".

The following morning Matthew rang the hospital and reception put him through to ICU. "Your wife is critical but stable sir".

"We are separated", said Matthew.

"Your wife is illegal over here we gather sir she will not be kept longer than is necessary arrangements will have to be made for her discharge".

"But we are not together haven't been for years I've a partner a daughter, has she not got a partner Dave?"

"Has she no friends?"

"A man brought her in yesterday, we cannot release details over the phone but we have reason to believe your ex wife was badly treated and for some time".

"Are there any relatives you could put us in contact with?"

"No there is nobody", said Matthew.

"The police are involved and due to your wife's alien status she will be deported as soon as possible". "Probably she will be transferred once stable to a hospital in Ireland". "Of course the next 24hrs will tell a lot so for now we will wait and see".

Matthew went out to the garden where Justine and Yvonne were playing with Triona. "Honey", said Matthew, "can we have a chat".

"Keep an eye on her Yvonne", said Justine, "as she walked into the house with Matthew".

"What is it?" Justine asked.

"It's Claire I rang the hospital she's critical but stable they say the next 24 hours will tell a lot". "They said she has been badly treated and for some time". "They say she will be deported once she's fit possibly to a hospital in Ireland". "She has no one Justine I feel I should go over there".

"What", said Justine? "If it was the other way around would she come to visit you?" "No Matthew she wouldn't she left with your best friend, she robbed you the woman doesn't give a shit about you". "You have a new life now you have me Yvonne Triona we are your family now". "The Claire's of this world will always be fine what about us?" "And what are you going to do over there?" "Go over to bring her back is it?"

"She has no one Justine you wouldn't leave a dog like that".

"Oh my god you want her back, back here is that what this is all about?"

"You want her back well I'm telling you this now It's me or her, make up your mind". "Justine it could never be a case of you or anyone I love you as soon as I can I'll marry you, you're the best thing that ever happened me". "I don't want to do anything to loose you if you feel that way I won't ring the hospital I'll leave well enough alone".

Justine didn't know what to say she was mad at Matthew why had he to ring that hospital. And then she began to think did she not say yesterday that she would support Matthew through this. Justine turned walked out into the garden picked up Triona in her arms and walked out the door. She walked and walked until it began to rain. She hadn't brought the pram Triona would be soaked she went in the first open door way she saw. It was Cakes and Things coffee shop. It was empty which was unusual these days. Justine went to the counter and got a coffee and an orange juice with a straw. She sat Triona in a baby chair and memories began to flow back. She remembered the day Matthew had met her here. When she didn't know where she would turn. She remembered the nauseating fear of the unknown. She remembered Matthew packing her stuff, organizing everything, and she knew what to do. Justine didn't finish her coffee she picked up Triona and got a taxi up home. Matthew sat at the kitchen table staring at the floor. He didn't know what to do but there was no way that a ghost from his past was going to come back and rob him of his life. He felt bad now but that would pass and he was sure Claire would be fine like Justine said the Claire's of this world were always fine. He never heard the door open or Justine go up stairs, he never heard her come back down stairs with the packed bags. Justine walked into the kitchen and wrapped her arms around Matthews's neck.

Matthew smiled, "hi honey he turned and looked out the door and saw the packed bag". De ja vu hit him like a rock and he froze in the chair.

"Matthew get up", said Justine.

"Justine no, no Justine", said Matthew.

"Come on", said Justine, "we have a plane to catch we are going to New York". Matthew threw his arms around Justine "you are amazing I thought you were leaving me". "Are we bringing Yvonne and Triona?"

"No Matthew we are just going ourselves". "I rang the hospital from Perpetual's they extubated Claire this morning and say she is doing ok". "She could be transferred to a regular ward tomorrow if she goes well tonight and the day after that she will be deported". "I've booked us into the Plaza for four nights but we could be home before then all going well". "Yvonne can mind Triona for the week and Perpetual will keep an eye on them".

"I've got to go pack Matthew stood up from the table and smiled there were two bags sitting at the door".

"I only have to walk out the door he laughed".

"Yeah come on we got to go".

As they sat on the plane Matthew thought of all the lonely nights at the start when he had felt like jumping on a plane and heading to America to Claire. He thought of the happiness he had that he could never have had with Claire and he felt angry. Anger at Claire for the way she had treated him. Anger at Claire for keeping his contact details like he owed her any kind of loyalty. For having him guilted into being responsible for her. Angry at the bond that existed between them despite his best efforts to break it. They landed in New York got a taxi to the Plaza took their Bags to their room came back down stairs and had dinner. After dinner they rang the hospital and were told that Claire had done very well and had been transferred to a ward.

"Justine", said Matthew, "I don't know if I want to see her I know it's the right thing to do but it's like this has made it all come back". "I feel so angry at her".

"Sure", said Justine, "we can go to the hospital talk with staff and if you want we need never see her".

The following morning at seven Justine and Matthew had breakfast and headed to the hospital. Their appointment was for eight thirty they were there for eight fifteen. The doctor walked in with a file.

"Mr. Ryan you are the next of kin I believe and who is this?"

"This is my partner Justine".

"And you are here to accompany the patient on her transfer to Ireland".

"Well we came anyway under the circumstances".

"You know what happened?" asked the doctor.

"No what?" Matthew asked, "all I know is that there was a question that Claire was badly treated, where was Dave during all this?"

"Dave Danaher", said the doctor, "it is he who treated your ex wife badly". "He was arrested I can't tell you anymore you will have to contact the detectives dealing with the case".

The doctor gave Matthew the number of the detective.

"What exactly do you need from me", Matthew asked the doctor.

"I needed you to give the consent that night and you did, to be honest ex wife and all I didn't expect to see you here".

"I need nothing from you but I'm sure your ex wife will be glad to see a friendly face". "We will go see the detective you have my details for billing thanks for seeing us". Justine and Matthew went to the station to see the detective. He brought them to a room and said Dave Danaher has been deported back home he was an illegal here. He pulled out photos and showed them to Matthew and Justine. They were of bruises cuts and injuries.

"I would have liked to hold on to that bastard but that's the way it is".

Justine looked whiter than white Matthew felt sick to his stomach. They got up and left the station.

"What now", asked Matthew?

"Will we go to the hospital?" Justine said.

Matthew and Justine walked into the hospital and got directions from reception they arrived into the ward and were directed to Claire's room. Matthew walked in behind Justine shaking he didn't know why. Claire looked up. She didn't know who the woman was through bruised eyes she could make out the shadow of a man behind her. She would know that shadow anywhere.

"Matthew", said Claire.

Matthew looked at her. Her swollen cut and bruised face. She looked emaciated and smaller than he remembered her. He walked over to the bed.

"Hello Claire, we have come to bring you home, this is Justine my partner we are going to bring you to stay with us until you are better".

Claire began to cry "I'm so sorry Matthew".

"It doesn't matter Claire", said Matthew, "it's all over now everything will be alright I promise".

"I can't expect you to do that I will be fine everything will work out".

"You're coming with us, said Justine, your coming with us and we are going to see your on your feet again".

"You can't look after yourself and you like this". "We have a mad house, said Matthew we have two girls". "Yvonne 18 and Triona 1 Mrs. O'Brien's crew are always in and out you remember Mrs. O'Brien surely".

"Yeah, said Claire, yeah I do". "Awe Matthew, said Claire, "I'm so sorry". "If there was anything I would change it would be the way I treated you".

"Don't be sorry", said Matthew, "if you hadn't done what you did I never would have gotten to know Justine I'm happier now than I ever was and things will be better for you to Claire".

"Things will get better".

Matthew turned around. "Come on Justine we are going to have to find someone to ask when Claire will be ready to come home".

They walked out of the room and were directed to the ward director.

"Claire can go whenever you like she will need a lot of rest and she has stitches to the abdomen that will need to be removed".

"Our GP can do that", said Matthew.

"There is just one thing said the nurse we told Claire this morning she's pregnant".

"Why that's great news said Justine".

"Yeah, said Matthew that will get her over this".

"Yeah but", said the nursing director.

"Don't worry", said Matthew, "everything will be sorted in that line once she gets home the GP will organize scans and all that".

The following morning Justine, Claire and Matthew sat on a plane home to Ireland. As the wheels of the plane hit the tarmac in Shannon Claire began to cry. They walked to the short term car park and drove the forty minutes to Nenagh. They were home a day earlier than expected Yvonne was in the sitting room with Triona Ciaran, Cian, Hanna and Mrs. O'Brien they turned around when the door opened.

"I better go", said Perpetual, "come on kids we will let them get settled in".

"Wait Mrs. O'Brien", said Claire.

"Look at you pet", said Mrs. O'Brien, "don't worry your home now we will all look after you".

"How can you say that", said Claire, "after the way I treated you?"

"Look how big Hanna's gotten, and you Ciaran you're practically a man".

"Look", said Mrs. O'Brien, "we will talk to you tomorrow, we are going to go and let you get settled".

"Ok", said Claire, "maybe we will have coffee some evening".

Mrs. O'Brien left Yvonne had gone out to the kitchen with Triona as she was crying. "I've frightened her", said Claire, "I look like the elephant woman".

"Never worry", said Justine, "the swelling will be gone down in a couple of days". Claire had left Ireland with three boxes of designer clothes and the guts of 200,000 euros she returned with the clothes on her back that were dirty and stained.

"I'll get you pajamas and you can go to bed", said Justine. "You need your rest".

"I have something I have to tell you and Matthew".

"Matthew held out his hand to Justine and she caught it".

"Yvonne can you give us a minute". Yvonne turned to leave.

"No", said Claire, "Yvonne too".

"Hi", she said to Yvonne extending her hand. "I'm Claire".

"Pleased to meet you", said Yvonne.

"I want to thank you all for having me in your home". "Justine you're a better woman than me there is no way in hell I would have a partner of mine bring his ex wife into my house". "I promise I won't be in the way and as soon as possible I will be on my feet and out of your way". "If I can do anything for ye let me know".

"Your suppose to be resting", said Matthew, "you've been through a lot".

"Yeah", said Justine.

"I treated you very badly Matthew I stole your money", Claire continued, "I never gave your feelings any regard", "I was rude to everyone". "I know how it feels to be treated like that now and I'm so sorry for how I treated you".

"Don't be upsetting yourself", said Justine, think of the baby".

"Oh my god", said Claire, "I thought I dreamed them telling me that I didn't dare hope". "It's true", said Matthew, "your pregnant".

"We will arrange for you to go to the doctor Monday and get sorted".

"Yvonne gave Claire a hug that's great news".

Claire winced her sides were sore.

"Oh sorry", said Yvonne.

"Come on", said Justine, "I'll get you a pajama and get some rest".

Claire walked after Justine stiff and sore and barely able to move. She was like a woman in her eighties. Matthew went next door to Perpetual Shelia was there.

"How is she they asked Matthew?"

"It wouldn't do ye any good to see her she's in bits".

"How could Dave have done this?"

"It's terrible", said Shelia, "but remember be careful there she nearly destroyed you once already".

"It's different now", said Matthew, "I have no feelings for her whatsoever". "I think it was an obsession I had with her". "I saw her as the embodiment of the way I wanted to portray my-self confident popular". "In Justine I found how to be happy to except myself for what I am because she accepted me for what I am". "And all of you we have all become so close and I wouldn't change things for the world Claire leaving me was the best thing in the world and there is no way I would want her back".

"Me and Justine are just doing what's right sure you wouldn't walk away from a dog in that state". "She's pregnant as well".

"Ah", said Perpetual, "sure that's great".

"Yeah", said Shelia, "the baby will get her through this".

Over in New York Shawn drove to JFK airport to start another day at work. He pulled the Escalade into the pick up bay and jumped out. There were a boy and girl sitting on the path smoking.

"You shouldn't be smoking here", Shawn said to them, "you'll get fined". "Is that your pram?"

"Yeah they replied putting out their cigarettes".

"Awe", said Shawn, "she's lovely a girl isn't she".

"Yeah they replied".

"Your Irish", said Shawn.

"Yes mister", said the girl, "do you know of any reasonable apartments to rent or good hostels or hotels that won't cost an arm and a leg".

"Over here to stay are we?" Shawn asked.

"Yeah they replied there's no work at home any more".

"That's terrible", said Shawn, "what age are you?"

"Eighteen," they replied.

"What part of Ireland ye from?"

"Limerick", they replied, "I'm Shawna, said the girl holding out her hand pleased to meet you".

"And I'm Darren", said the boy.

"Nice to meet ye", said Shawn.

"Can you tell us where to get a bus or train or something into New York?" Shawna asked.

"Hold on a minute", said Shawn. "Firstly I'm Shawn".

"Ha, ha", said Shawna, "we've nearly got the same name".

"It must be fate", said Darren.

"Maybe, said Shawn, "now firstly I think I know where there might be a furnished beautiful apartment going a begging". "Two bedrooms and not too dear". "Also I know a diner that might need a waitress near there". "I've got to pick up customers here jump in you can sit up front with me". Where is your luggage?

Darren pointed to a trolley with two large cases.

"Is that it?", Shawn asked, "pop it in the boot and get yourselves and the baby in the car".

"What's her name", asked Shawn?

"Amelia", said Shawna.

"Thanks very much for all this", said Darren as they packed their stuff into the boot.

"No worries", said Shawn, "I've got to go in and collect customers bring them back to the hotel".

Shawna, Darren and baby Amelia got into the car. Shawn opened the door.

"Darren see that button press it". "It's the screen between the front and the back". "I can't have the customers see ye". "If they see I'm carrying ye for free they might not want to pay either".

"Jesus no", said Darren, "we are going to pay you, we couldn't have that and you doing so much for us".

"We can talk about that later, am in to get the customers be back in a minute".

Shawn went into the airport and collected a French couple. He dropped them to their hotel and then drove Shawna and Darren to the all American diner. Jamine sat in a booth drinking coffee and reading the paper. Shawn walked over to him.

"Hi there", said Jamine, "looking up from the paper and who do you have with you and who is this little girl".

"This is Shawna and Darren and little baby Amelia from Ireland looking for an apartment".

"And Shawna would be interested in a waitress job if one is going".

"Oh I see", said Jamine, "well maybe this will be ok". "Here are the keys Shawn he threw the keys to Claire's and Dave's apartment to him"." I'll give ye the first week for free, said Jamine".

"What's the snag", asked Darren.

"There are things in there belonging to other people pack them up and leave them in the hall". "I can't face going over there Shawn". "That's why the place is sitting there idle for so long". "Couldn't head in there after all that happened".

"What's wrong with the place?" Shawna asked.

"Nothing", said Jamine, "it's just the last couple that were in there left in a hurry and the place is a mess", "Rosie he shouted to a girl behind the counter give them out a roll of black sacks".

"We can do that for you mister no problem".

Shawn took them up the stairs and into the apartment.

"Shawna smiled it's beautiful, it's perfect".

"Hold on a minute", said Darren. "How much is the rent?"

"$150 a week don't worry ye will be well able to afford it".

"We have a thousand euro", said Shawna, "how soon can I start work do you think?" "Straight away I would reckon but would you not like a week off to get settled in?"

"No", said Shawna, "I'll start as soon as".

"Okay I'll take you back over to Jamine as soon as you have the clothes and stuff packed up". "Here's my number I've got to head work will be looking for me".

Shawn patted Amelia on the head and left.

"Darren are you tired no pet he replied not a bit". "Oh Shawna we have been so lucky we have met the soundest people in the world".

"I know Darren how will we ever repay them".

"Darren we have the travel cot for Amelia and we will sleep in the sleeping bags I don't want to sleep in someone else's sheets".

"I agree", said Darren, "why don't we go out find a take away come back put Amelia to bed and then we will pack all the other peoples stuff".

"That's a great idea said Shawna lets head".

Darren carried Amelia down the stairs and Shawna carried the buggy. They found a Chinese on the corner and they feed Amelia the baby food that Shawna had in her hand bag and gave her one of the pre prepared bottles. They returned to the apartment. Amelia was asleep in the buggy and never woke when Darren carried her upstairs. They put her in the travel cot and covered her with her blankie.

"Fine", said Darren, "I'll take one bedroom you take the other and we will do the living room kitchen together".

"Dead on said Shawna".

"Jesus", said Darren, "all the clothes are cut up in here its all girls clothes".

"The clothes in here are fine they are mans". "Ah well", said Shawna, "I know something bad must of happened here they said they left in a hurry but that doesn't mean it won't be lucky for us".

"Yeah", said Darren, "we have been lucky even if it's cos of someone else's misfortune".

Darren froze Shawna screamed.

"What is it?" Darren shouted as he ran across into the room to Shawna. She stood there holding up loads and loads of money.

"Ring Shawn, Darren".

Darren rang Shawn straight away he was there with Jamine in an hour. They had everything packed and in the hall.

"So", said Jamine walking in, "what's the panic I'd swear this place is cursed the little baby is ok is she".

"Yeah", said Shawna, "she is fast asleep".

"Come with me", said Darren.

He took them into the room; Shawna found this box full of money in amongst clothes. "Jesus Christ" said Shawn.

"I bet it was amongst men's clothes", said Jamine, "and that bastard had her worked into the ground".

"We will tell you all some day", said Shawn, "when you're older" and laughed.

"What will we do?" Jamine asked.

"I'll ring Aunty Perpetual".

Shawn rang his Aunty it was morning in Ireland the phone was answered straight away. "Oh my God, oh my God was all Perpetual could say as Shawn told her". "Ciaran run out get me Justine or Matthew".

Matthew came running in the door Yvonne after him.

"It's ok said Perpetual nothing's wrong its good news for a change". "It's Shawn in America here will you talk to him?"

Matthew was in shock.

"No, no Shawn she has not opened a bank account yet but I'll give you my account number if it's ok with you if you'd trust me?"

"Well, said Shawn, after what she did to you, you came got her I'd say we can trust you".

"Can I take your number and get back to you? I want to tell Claire. I think it's only right that she give some money to that young couple".

"How much money is in it?"

"$300,000" said Shawn.

"Oh my God", said Matthew, "I'll talk to her and ring you right back is that ok?"

"It's perfect".

"Oh my God", said Claire crying. "Oh my God I don't want it". "I don't want it".

"Listen here now", said Justine, "he treated you badly". "He spent all that money you took with you".

Claire looked at Matthew, "but that was Matthew's money I stole".

"That's over and done with now", said Matthew, "that loan is nearly paid back and no offence Claire but leaving me was the biggest favor you ever did me it was worth it". Claire laughed.

"Tell him to give $5,000 to that young couple and tell him to thank them from me for their honesty". "Also tell Shawn to take whatever he wants and Jamine too".

Matthew rang Shawn back and passed on Claire's message.

"We will take out the money for Darren and Shawna they have a little baby this will be a great help to them but we don't want any of that bastard's money".

"We want no money either", said Shawna.

"No", said Darren, "you both have been so good to us we feel like we know ye forever not just a few hours". "We need nothing your friendship is more than enough", said Shawna.

Jamine hugged her, "I think we are going to get on great". "Yeah", said Shawn.

"No, no", said Matthew, "I have to insist on that couple taking the money they could have said nothing and no one would be any the wiser". "Claire really wants them to have it, it means a lot to her".

"She has nothing and she's pregnant they don't realize what they have done".

"Ok, said Shawn did ye hear that".

Darren and Shawna nodded. They hung up from Matthew. Shawna turned to Jamine. "Can I still have the job at the diner?"

"Of course you can but do you still want to start straight away after that windfall?" "Yeah", said Shawna, "I do".

"Start Tuesday so", said Jamine.

"Thank you so much", said Shawna.

"I don't want to be rude or pushy or anything", said Darren, "but if ye hear of anything going for me would you let me know?"

"What can you do son", asked Shawn?

"I've just finished my carpentry apprenticeship", said Darren.

"My brother is a contractor I'll get on to him and let you know".

"Oh thank you so much", said Darren.

"You will both have to come to dinner Sunday, said Shawna bring your families we want to thank you".

Jamine and Shawn smiled.

"You know", said Shawn, "I carried loads of shit up the stairs for that last pair and all the thanks I got was being told I need not think I would be getting paid". "They even complained about the fare here when I moved their stuff".

They all laughed.

"Ah", said Jamine, "like I said earlier we are going to get along just fine".

"I've two kids said Shawn".

"Oh that's great are they little they can play with Amelia I know she is little yet".

"They are three and five they will enjoy the baby".

"I've a wife and two too but mine are teenagers twelve and fifteen", said Jamine.

"Are you sure about this?"

"Yeah certain", said Shawna, "if you wouldn't mind coming I'd love to cook for ye". Ok so, said Jamine, "but I'll bring the desert from the diner".

"Yeah", said Shawn, "and I'll bring the starter I do a mean Cesar salad".

"Have you all the stuff packed already?"

"We do we have a bag over there but it's the food from the fridge and presses".

"I'll take that with me too it can go in the skip out back at the diner".

"Thanks, said Shawna." "So what time suits you Sunday could you do one o clock or is it too early".

"Sounds fine to me", said Shawn, "me too said Jamine".

Jamine and Shawn left and Darren helped them take the bags down stairs.

"That bag is men's clothes and they are ok". "The others are women's clothes but they are all torn up even the shoes are broken".

"Thanks Darren", said Jamine, "we couldn't face doing that ourselves". "We will take the men's clothes to the YMCA, and the others can go in the skip with the food".

The following morning Shawn lodged the money to his account had it converted and transferred into Matthews account. Matthew took Claire to the bank where she opened an account and they transferred the money in there. Jamine and Shawn refused to take any of the money. Claire rang them to thank them. She tried to convince them to let her give them some of the money but they wouldn't hear of it.

"I'm not forgetting all you have done for me; I will find some way to repay you", Claire insisted.

Claire stayed with Matthew and Justine until the month before she was due to give birth. One Monday morning when she Justine, Perpetual, Yvonne, Anna and Maria were having coffee Maria told them that she was going home there was a boom.

She was going to rent her home here she missed home too much she wanted to go back and as soon as possible.

"We will miss you", said Shelia.

"Definitely", said Perpetual, "but surely you'll come back visit us?"

"Of course", said Maria.

"But listen Claire I don't want to push you but would you rent my house I want to see how things go at home before I sell".

"Oh my God", said Claire, "I was thinking but I didn't like to ask".

"Only of course", she turned to Justine, "if I won't be too close for comfort".

"Of course not", said Justine.

"Yeah", said Yvonne, "and I want the baby close you promised I'd be godmother remember?"

"I do", said Claire.

"I don't want to be pushy Maria but when do you leave?"

"Friday", said Maria, "I'm packed and all".

"How much do you want?"

"Six hundred euros a month to cover the mortgage is that ok?"

"Perfect", said Claire, "and how much for the deposit?"

"I don't need a deposit", said Maria, "I will leave you my bank details and you can pay the money in there".

Yvonne and Justine helped Claire to pack. In honesty there wasn't too much to take, just clothes that Claire had gotten since she came home from pennies and dunes.

"I never thought I'd see the day you'd wear clothes from dunes and pennies", Matthew said.

"I was such a fool", said Claire.

Claire had nothing bought for the baby. "I'll get it when I come home", she said, "in case anything goes wrong".

On the morning Maria left Claire gave her a card. Maria never opened it until she was on the plane it was seven hundred euros.

Treat this as a deposit a non refundable one the card read. Thank you so much. Love Claire.

Maria smiled and to think I used hate her. The following morning Claire went to the bank. She lodged a years rent into a separated account and organized a direct debit for the money to be paid to Maria. She left three thousand in the account to get the baby stuff. She lodged the rest into Matthews account. Claire left the bank feeling great in the first time in forever. She went to the nursery shop and bought a cot pram and bedding and blankets. She asked them to hold onto them in the shop until she had delivered. They didn't mind at all. Next she took the list for the baby from her hand bag and bought everything she needed for the baby and herself and a sports bag to pack them all in. She went home and washed the baby grows she had bought for the child and the nightdresses and pajamas she had bought herself. Yvonne called over with Triona and Hanna. Claire gave her the receipts for the baby stuff and fifty euros. I want to ask you a favor see when I go into hospital to have the child could you collect this stuff. Of course, said Yvonne. Are you sure you don't mind? I'm certain, said Yvonne. She packed her bag and left it ready at the door. A week later to the day, she went into labor at three in the morning. This was something she wanted to do for herself.

She rang the ambulance "it's not an emergency" she said, "don't bother with any sirens the neighbors are asleep".

The ambulance arrived at three fifteen. Claire was at the door bag in hand she locked the door and they helped her into the ambulance. She delivered a baby boy at four thirty in the morning. She called him Joy. At nine in the morning she rang everyone and told them. Justine, Matthew, Triona, Yvonne, Perpetual, Shelia, Seorsha, Hanna, Ciaran, and Cian all arrived laden with gifts. Two days later Claire arrived home with baby Joy. Yvonne had brought home all the baby stuff. The house was full even Tom, Catriona, Ashley and Adrian were there. You know Matthew, said Adrian I have kept all those love notes you sent Claire with those flowers. They are in the top drawer of my desk. Matthew looked at Adrian and laughed that's where they should stay, that's where they should stay.

Matthew looked around the room at all the happy smiling faces. All these people intrinsically connected like the fine threads of a spider's web. Bound together through good times and bad he was to them as they were to him unconditionally yours.